–The–
Gold Miners' Rescue

Trailblazer Books

HISTORIC CHARACTERS	TITLE
Gladys Aylward	Flight of the Fugitives
Mary McLeod Bethune	Defeat of the Ghost Riders
William & Catherine Booth	Kidnapped by River Rats
Charles Loring Brace	Roundup of the Street Rovers
William Bradford	The Mayflower Secret
John Bunyan	Traitor in the Tower
Amy Carmichael	The Hidden Jewel
Peter Cartwright	Abandoned on the Wild Frontier
Maude Cary	Risking the Forbidden Game
George Washington Carver	The Forty-Acre Swindle
Frederick Douglass	Caught in the Rebel Camp
Elizabeth Fry	The Thieves of Tyburn Square
Chief Spokane Garry	Exiled to the Red River
Barbrooke Grubb	Ambushed in Jaguar Swamp
Jonathan & Rosalind Goforth	Mask of the Wolf Boy
Sheldon Jackson	The Gold Miners' Rescue
Adoniram & Ann Judson	Imprisoned in the Golden City
Festo Kivengere	Assassins in the Cathedral
David Livingstone	Escape From the Slave Traders
Martin Luther	Spy for the Night Riders
Dwight L. Moody	Danger on the Flying Trapeze
Lottie Moon	Drawn by a China Moon
Samuel Morris	Quest for the Lost Prince
George Müller	The Bandit of Ashley Downs
John Newton	The Runaway's Revenge
Florence Nightingale	The Drummer Boy's Battle
John G. Paton	Sinking the Dayspring
William Penn	Hostage on the Nighthawk
Joy Ridderhof	Race for the Record
Nate Saint	The Fate of the Yellow Woodbee
Rómulo Sauñe	Blinded by the Shining Path
William Seymour	Journey to the End of the Earth
Menno Simons	The Betrayer's Fortune
Mary Slessor	Trial by Poison
Hudson Taylor	Shanghaied to China
Harriet Tubman	Listen for the Whippoorwill
William Tyndale	The Queen's Smuggler
John Wesley	The Chimney Sweep's Ransom
Marcus & Narcissa Whitman	Attack in the Rye Grass
David Zeisberger	The Warrior's Challenge

-The-
Gold Miners' Rescue

Dave & Neta Jackson

Illustrated by Julian Jackson

CASTLE
ROCK
CREATIVE
Evanston, Illinois 60202

Published by Castle Rock Creative, Inc.
Evanston, Illinois 60202

Previously published by
Bethany House, a division of
Baker Publishing Group

Unless otherwise noted, all Scripture quotations are from the King James Version of the Bible

Inside illustrations by Julian Jackson
Cover illustration by Catherine Reishus McLaughlin

ISBN: 978-1-939445-27-8

Printed in the United States of America

For a complete listing of
books by Dave and Neta Jackson visit
www.daveneta.com
www.trailblazerbooks.com

Three significant elements in this story are fictional.

First, the order of some events during 1897-1898 were juggled as follows: The 109th General Assembly of the Presbyterian Church where Jackson was elected moderator took place from May 20-21, 1897, *before* he made that year's trip to Alaska. Also, Jackson made his rounds to the northern mission stations and schools *after* his reconnaissance trip up the Yukon River, not before.

Second, while Captain Michael Healy and his famous revenue cutter, the *Bear*, had almost become Jackson's private transport in Alaskan waters (as portrayed in this story), Captain Healy was actually court-martialed for his drinking problem and suspended from service in 1896, just before the start of this story. Nevertheless, we included him in this book because he was such an integral part of Alaska's and Sheldon Jackson's history. His license was reinstated in 1900 when he was given command of a new cutter, the *McCullock*.

Finally, although Jackson founded the Sitka Industrial and Training School (as well as many other schools) and regularly oversaw its operation, there is no record of him stopping there in 1897. But in order to show the breadth and nature of Jackson's work and especially his famous trip to Lapland to rescue the gold miners, we created a fictional student, Adam Christian, and the scholarship award.

As far as we know, we (Dave and Neta Jackson) are not related to Sheldon Jackson.

Dave and Neta Jackson, husband and wife writing team, are the authors or coauthors of more than 120 books that have sold over 2.5 million copies. They are best known for the 40-volume Trailblazer Books series for young readers and the Hero Tales series for families. Adults love their Yada Yada Prayer Group series, House of Hope series, Harry Bentley series, and Windy City Neighbors series along with numerous nonfiction books. They make their home in the Chicago area. Find out more about them at www.daveneta.com.

CONTENTS

1. Graduation 9
2. Bottled Trouble 21
3. The Ghost Village 32
4. Reindeer Station 43
5. "Gold! Gold! Gold!" 55
6. Stranded 68
7. The Whiskey Barrel Kayak 79
8. Glory Days 91
9. Journey to the End of the Earth 102
10. The World Watches 112
11. Stuck in Skagway 123
12. "Maybe for This You Were Born" 133

More About Sheldon Jackson 142

Chapter 1

Graduation

WAITING IN LINE WHILE all the other boys went into the little room to be interviewed by Dr. Sheldon Jackson had been like waiting for ice on the Yukon River to break up in the spring. But it had been Adam's choice to slip to the back of the line and let the other thirteen boys go first. *If I'm the last one Dr. Jackson speaks to*, thought Adam, *he'll remember me best.*

In his four years at Sitka Industrial and Training School, Adam Christian had never met Dr. Jackson. But today, Alaska's agent of education had come for the graduation ceremony, and—most important to Adam—he had come to announce the winner of the scholarship award. The winner would travel with Dr. Jackson all

the way to the great white chief's village of Washington, D.C., in the United States.

As Adam waited, he brushed a speck of lint off the front of his black suit and straightened his starched white shirt. He was a handsome lad with square features that were not so flat as the Eskimos along Alaska's northwestern coast nor so hawkish as the Tlingit and Tsimshian Indians near Sitka. He was a Tananan from the Yukon River. But he would not call that home much longer if he won the award. With his fingers he combed his thick black hair off his forehead and stood straighter.

If he won, he would escape Alaska, get away from the frozen tundra, and make a new start in the white man's world.

The contestants for the award came from all the Indian and Eskimo schools that Dr. Jackson had founded throughout Alaska, but Adam was sure the winner would be selected from the Sitka School—after all, it was the oldest and best school—and he had worked very hard to be its best student.

Today he would find out if he had reached his goal, and he was next in line.

Waiting, waiting, waiting.

"Adam Christian," the voice of Superintendent Kelly, his Sitka schoolmaster, came through the closed door. Mustering all his confidence, Adam turned the door handle and entered.

Three men were standing behind a table. The one on the right was Superintendent Kelly, with his high forehead, beady eyes, and a black beard so full that the students sometimes joked that he had no mouth. Of course, Adam already knew him. But the other two men were unfamiliar.

The tall, muscular man on the left drew Adam's attention first. He had a huge walrus mustache and short black hair streaked with gray. His nose was wide, and his skin was as dark and weathered as any Indian's, yet he wore the uniform of a ship's captain. For just a moment the man's green eyes smiled at Adam from under their heavy lids; then his face resumed the sad look of someone who had seen far too much trouble.

But it was the little man in the center who reached his hand out. Without meaning to, Adam stared. *Could this be Dr. Jackson?* Finally, he grasped the man's hand, shaking it firmly... though not for too long. But he's so small, thought Adam. *Everyone speaks of Dr. Jackson as a great man. I thought he'd be a big man, but he's not even as tall as I am.*

Indeed, Sheldon Jackson was a mere five feet two inches tall. He wore platform shoes and—except when indoors—a high-crowned derby hat. In every way, he attempted to give himself the appearance of a little more height than God had given him. His stiff white beard had been trimmed to a point below his chin, and he wore steel-rimmed, oval-shaped spectacles, not much larger than his intense blue eyes. Sharp eyes, tiny spectacles, pointed beard, and the frown lines between his up-slanting eyebrows—he looked like a hawk ready to attack.

In an unusually friendly voice Dr. Jackson said,

11

"Adam Christian, please sit down, my boy." Then he and the other men took their seats.

But Adam remained standing stiffly before them. He focused his eyes on a picture on the wall behind the three men. It was a cross-stitch, needlework sampler of the alphabet with some flowers around

the edge. In his nervousness, Adam couldn't help but read the letters one at a time.

"I see in your records," said Dr. Jackson, shuffling some papers on the table before him, "that you came from the Tananan people up along the Yukon River. What is your Indian name?"

Adam dropped his head and mumbled, "Gnob."

"Did you say, 'Gnob'?" interrupted the tall, dark man on the left. "Wasn't that the name of a Tanana chief some time back?"

Adam nodded and said, "My grandfather."

"Well," said Dr. Jackson, "but now you go by the name of..." He glanced again at the paper in front of him. "Adam Christian. Did one of the priests at the Episcopal mission there give you that name?"

"No, sir," said Adam, still staring straight ahead. "I chose it for myself."

"Is that so? And what made you choose such an interesting name?"

"Since Adam in the Bible was the first man," explained the boy, "I wanted to be the first man from my Tananan tribe to make it in the outside world. I also wanted everyone to know that I am a Christian. So I am Adam Christian."

"Well, now," said Jackson, puffing out his chest like a bantam rooster and turning to the large man by his side, "what do you think of that, Captain Healy? I told you some of these Indians have ambition."

Captain Michael Healy, thought Adam. *Of course that's who the big man is.* Adam had never met the captain, but everyone in Alaska had heard of him. He captained the revenue cutter the *Bear* along Alaska's coast, stopping poachers from killing seals, walrus, and whales out of season. He and the *Bear* had rescued many fishermen. And he was always arresting the crew of some ship trying to smuggle whiskey and rum to the Eskimos and Indians. Adam had seen a sparkling three-masted cutter with one smokestack anchored in Sitka's harbor earlier that morning. It must have been the *Bear*.

Adam stole a glance at Dr. Jackson. The little man had an impish grin on his face as he looked over the top of his spectacles at the captain. The boy's hopes rose. He straightened his shoulders again. Maybe he *was* making a good impression on the doctor.

Captain Healy, however, turned disinterestedly away and pulled at the right corner of his mustache. "You know, Doctor," he said with a sigh, "I've never doubted for a moment the ambition of these young people. The only question is, in what direction will you point it?"

"Indeed, indeed so," said Dr. Jackson with the confidence of the first robin in spring. "And that's why I offered this scholarship. I knew any number of boys would work hard for a trip to Washington." He turned back to Adam, who quickly averted his eyes back up to the needlework on the wall. "What do you say, son—is that something you'd like?"

"Oh yes, sir. I would like it very much." He paused for a moment, trying to think of what he could say that would demonstrate his seriousness. "I would consider it an important educational opportunity," he said, pronouncing the big words with care.

"Very good, very good," said Jackson, rubbing his two small hands rapidly together as though he were generating heat. "But tell me, why didn't you go to the St. James Mission school near your home on the Yukon? Don't you miss your family?"

Adam had answered this question many times for his teachers and others at Sitka who wondered why he traveled over seven hundred miles south when another school was close to home. But this time his answer had to do more than satisfy someone's curiosity. This time he would show the only person who really mattered what he intended to do with his life. He looked directly at Dr. Jackson and said, "I came to the Sitka Industrial and Training School—the school you started, sir—because it is the best school in Alaska, and I wanted the best training so I could become a success in the United States."

At this comment, Dr. Jackson stared off into space, his crooked smile almost erasing the frown lines between his eyebrows. The windows of the Sitka school had been opened to let in the fresh mountain air on that relatively warm Friday afternoon of June 11, 1897. Finally Captain Healy broke the silence.

"Yes, it's good to want to be a success," he said. "We all want that for you—and the other students, as well. But why not be a success among your Tananan people? Why do you want to go to the States?"

Adam shrugged. "Why would I want to go back to my tribe?"

"Don't you want to help your people—teach them what you have learned here?" asked the captain.

Adam hesitated slightly. "I... don't want to live like an Indian," he murmured in a voice so quiet it could barely be heard, even in the small room.

"Of course not," put in Dr. Jackson. "And you would never again live like an Indian, not after what you have learned here. You'll help your people by becoming a success wherever you go. Maybe you'll become a... teacher or even a missionary like Peter McKay or Rev. Edward Marsden—now, they were Indians like yourself. I'm sure that would make your family very proud. You know Rev. Marsden, don't you? He did very well at Marietta College and Lane Theological Seminary. And I'm confident that the mission board will send him as the new pastor to the village of Saxman by next summer. Think of that, son. You could follow in his footsteps."

Adam took a breath. "But I don't want to follow in his footsteps," he said stubbornly. He wanted to sound grateful, but he had his own goals. He had never met Edward Marsden personally, but he had heard enough about him around Sitka. The full-blooded native was often mentioned as one of the school's model graduates from years past. But as Dr. Jackson had just noted, Edward Marsden was going *back* to live among his Indian people, something Adam had no intention of doing. "What I want to do," said Adam in a quiet voice, "is become a success like *you*, Dr. Jackson."

A warm smile spread slowly across Dr. Jackson's

sharp features. "Well," he said, looking down at his papers again, "can you recite something for me, son? I need to know whether you have a good grasp of the king's English."

"But, Sheldon, whatever for?" said Captain Healy impatiently. "Let the lad go. You have his records... along with the records of all the others. Obviously he understands and speaks English well enough to get—"

"'The Lord is my shepherd,'" interrupted Adam. "'I shall not want. He maketh me to lie down in green pastures: he leadeth me beside the still waters. He restoreth my soul: he leadeth me—'"

"That'll do. That'll do," said Captain Healy, waving his left hand before his face as though brushing away a mosquito. "We've been here all afternoon, Sheldon. Why must this boy give us a recitation?"

"I need to *know*," said Dr. Jackson in a quiet but determined voice. "I need to know how he might come across... in public."

Adam spoke up. "I speak good English because I am the only Tananan here. No one else knows my tribal language, so I learned English quickly—more quickly than the other boys," he added, hoping Dr. Jackson would take note of his intelligence. He paused and looked from one man to the other. When no one said anything for a moment, Adam continued reciting Psalm 23. "'...he leadeth me in the paths of righteousness—'"

"Good heavens." Healy threw up his hands and hissed through his lips like steam leaking from a ship's boiler. "Must I also endure a sermon? I haven't

17

been drinking that much on this trip, but you'll try anything to convert me, won't you, Sheldon?" He stopped, then suddenly twisted in his chair to face Sheldon Jackson and slammed his huge right fist into the palm of his left hand. "That's it! Isn't it?" he said with a look of wonderment on his face. "I can't believe it, Sheldon. You *will* try anything! You're planning a circus. You want to parade one of these poor fools in front of your Presbyterian missionary societies in the States so you can raise more money."

"Well, what if I do? They deserve to know that their contributions have been wisely spent." Jackson's voice was tense, but his tone changed to polite gentleness when he said, "Thank you, Adam. I trust that will be all. We'll see you tonight at the graduation."

That evening, with the summer sun still bright over the many small islands in Sitka Bay and the forested mountains rising steeply to snowy peaks behind the school, the graduating class of fourteen boys and five girls marched toward the small campus chapel. A light breeze slid down from the mountains behind the school, bringing with it the scent of cedar and pine, of damp moss in the shadows and dashing ice-cold brooks.

Inside the crowded chapel awaited the younger students, a few of the leading citizens from town, and the proud parents of the graduates—all, that is, except Adam's parents. But he didn't care. This was still an evening to remember.

The graduates walked somberly down the aisle and onto the platform while the little pump organ wheezed and whined its way through all five verses of "O God, Our Help in Ages Past." Then there were introductions by Superintendent Kelly and a speech by Dr. Jackson, but Adam was too excited to pay attention. He already knew that he was going to graduate. The only question was, would he win the award?

The graduation ceremony dragged on until Superintendent Kelly began reading the names of the graduates. Each one walked forward to receive a diploma and shake the superintendent's and Dr. Jackson's hands. When Adam's name was called, he tried to be as dignified as everyone else, but he felt like thousands of mosquitoes were buzzing inside him.

He watched Dr. Jackson's face as they shook hands. The doctor smiled and nodded to him, but it was nothing different than how he had greeted each of the other students. Adam felt uneasy as he made his way back to his place at the back of the platform. If Dr. Jackson had selected him for the award, wouldn't he have announced it when Adam came forward? Or if that was not the time for the announcement, wouldn't he have at least revealed his pleasure somehow to Adam when they shook hands?

Adam watched more carefully as the last two girls and one boy were called forward for their diplomas. But Dr. Jackson's response to them was no different than he had received. His heart sank. It was all over. He hadn't been selected for the award.

Probably Dr. Jackson had decided on someone from one of the other schools.

It had all been a waste. Why had he allowed himself to dream such big dreams? It was foolish to pin all his hopes on one thing. Now he would have to go back to his village.

Just then Adam caught sight of a movement out of the corner of his eye. Over to the left side of the stage, behind the edge of a curtain out of sight of the audience, stood Captain Healy, his arms folded across his chest and his feet set wide apart as though he were on the deck of a pitching ship. He nodded ever so slightly when he saw Adam looking at him, and suddenly Adam was convinced that he had been the person who blocked his selection for the award.

That had to be it. He thought back over the interview and remembered that Healy and Jackson disagreed over him for some reason. Whatever it was, Healy must have talked Dr. Jackson out of choosing him for the award. A bitterness seized Adam as he stared at the rugged sea captain.

But the man was nodding at Adam. His eyes got big, and he pointed with little jerking motions toward the front of the platform. The audience was clapping, and the boy next to Adam nudged him.

"Adam Christian," Dr. Jackson was saying, "would you please come forward?"

In utter surprise, Adam put a hand to his chest and looked from side to side.

"Yes, you, my boy. You have won the scholarship award. Come forward and say something to the people."

Chapter 2

Bottled Trouble

WHEN ADAM LEFT THE BOYS' DORMITORY the next morning, a gray fog lay over Sitka Bay like a blanket of damp cotton. Hesitant shadows of campus buildings and trees appeared and faded from view through the drifting mist. The scent of kelp, dead fish, rocky tide pools, and mud flats filled the damp air with a sharp tang. Adam could hear the gentle *lap, lap* of small waves on the stony beach and the slow, steady bong of the buoys guarding the offshore islands. Mournful cries from sea gulls split these rhythms as they dove and swooped through the ground-hugging clouds... somehow without colliding.

From out of the gloom ahead of Adam, the shape of a man appeared, rolling slightly from side to side with a sailor's gait as he walked slowly toward the dining hall. Adam hurried to catch up with him.

"Captain Healy?" he said.

The man turned and glanced at Adam without a smile. The collar of his sea coat was turned up against the damp, and the faint smell of whiskey surrounded him. *Why would anyone drink this early in the day?* wondered Adam.

"Will we be sailing today?" Adam asked, trying to sound lighthearted in case the captain was in a foul mood.

The captain looked up at the tall pine tree under which they were walking. Its trunk and upper branches disappeared in the fog. "I should hope so," he said without seeming upset. "This'll burn off in an hour or so, and if we don't pull anchor today, that preacher man Jackson is likely to object to sailing on Sunday." He chuckled to himself. "But once we're at sea, what can he do? However," the captain added with a frown as they walked along, "I don't think the doctor was planning to take you along with him today. He has to make his annual rounds of the villages and schools up the coast. We won't be back this way to pick you up until..." He touched each of the fingers on his left hand with his thumb, counting. "Until next September at the earliest."

"September?" Adam gulped.

"Mmm-hmm. At least that long. Heard him say he has to make a trip up the Yukon River—something about the secretary of agriculture asking him to explore the land to see if it can be cultivated—though only heaven knows why anyone would want to settle that far north." He looked down at Adam as though seeing him for the first time. "Oh—sorry, son. Forgot that's where you're from. Didn't mean to speak poorly of your homeland, but the idea of farming up there just doesn't make much sense to me."

Adam shrugged. His mind was on the disappointment of not going with Dr. Jackson that very day. What would he do all summer? He didn't want to work around the school or go up to Skagway to get a job helping those foolish miners carry their gear over the Chilkoot Pass. He had heard there was plenty of work and good money to be made from the gold-crazed men on their way to the Klondike, but it was likely to get stolen the next day.

Reports had been coming in for the last few months that gold had been found along the upper Yukon River, and Skagway—the town through which many miners traveled to get to the gold fields—was getting wild. Each day, it seemed, a new saloon opened, and fights and shootings, scams and robberies, were as common as snowflakes in a blizzard. Reports had it that there was no decent place to sleep and no food worth eating.

Adam was already smart enough to realize that such an insane race for riches would not get him what he really wanted. He wanted the kind of success and opportunity that would last, the kind Dr. Jackson had. Working for those stampeding miners, carrying their supplies up the steps hacked in the ice to the windy, treacherous pass was not worth any amount of money they'd pay. One slip, and he'd be dead. One day's work, and he'd be exhausted. One week's pay, and he'd be a target for robbers.

It wasn't worth it.

As they reached the dining hall, Adam suddenly had a more hopeful idea. "Captain Healy," he said, "if Dr. Jackson is going up the Yukon to look at the land, then he probably needs someone who knows the area, maybe someone who can speak the Tananan language, don't you think?"

The captain grinned under his big mustache, and small, friendly lines appeared at the edges of his eyes. "You might have something there," he chuckled as he held the door open for Adam and a couple other boys who had caught up to them. He looked around the room with its rows of tables and benches. "He's over there talking to your teacher, Mr. Kelly. Why don't you go ask him? I'll be along in a minute once I get some coffee."

As soon as Adam sat down on the bench across from Dr. Jackson and Superintendent Kelly, the doctor said, "Good morning, Adam. Are you looking forward to going to Washington with me next fall?"

"Yes, indeed, sir," said Adam. "But Captain Healy said you were going north first to look for good farmland along the Yukon. I could help you with that since that's where I'm from."

Dr. Jackson frowned. "Healy told you that? He shouldn't be so loose-lipped. We can't have every little expedition blabbed about. There are ears, you know—ears of people who might try to take advantage of news like that."

Even Superintendent Kelly looked puzzled, so lowering his voice and leaning forward, Dr. Jackson explained. "The secretary of agriculture asked me to make a trip up the Yukon this year to see if there is any decent agricultural land along that river. There have always been trappers in that region, but I suppose he's thinking about settlement now that miners are pouring in. It'll be a flood if they make a big strike. But I know he doesn't want his plans spread around. Speculators are likely to take advantage of them—buy up the land or get a corner on the riverboat transportation or who knows what else. One never knows. So just keep the purpose of this trip to yourselves." He leaned back as if finalizing his statement.

"As for myself," Dr. Jackson continued, "I've been thinking about establishing some new reindeer stations inland, maybe at St. James Mission—near where you're from, Adam."

"Sounds like a good idea," offered Adam, trying to sound helpful. "We hunt caribou, and they're kind of alike, aren't they?"

"Indeed. They're almost the same animal, son. The caribou are wild, while the reindeer have been domesticated. Reindeer can even be trained to pull sleds and carry packs. The Lapps do it all the time."

"Lapps?" said Adam.

"Yes, the people from Lapland." The doctor looked at Superintendent Kelly with a concerned frown. "Don't you teach these boys geography?"

"Of course," Kelly said with irritation. Turning to Adam, he prodded, "You know, Lapland. It's in Scandinavia, the northern part of Norway, Sweden, and Finland."

"And Russia," corrected Dr. Jackson. "We've even brought some Lapps over here to teach the Eskimos how to take care of the reindeer we imported from Siberia."

Adam nodded. "What I'm wondering is, can I come with you up the Yukon? I could show you around—where I used to live. I know that country."

"I'm sure you do, but I wasn't thinking of picking you up until I'm on my way back to the States. It's a mighty long trip."

"I know," said Adam. "I have traveled it four times."

"But, Adam," said Superintendent Kelly, "you did not go by sea and river—why, we're talking close to two thousand miles."

"Over three thousand," corrected Dr. Jackson. He looked at Adam, knitted his brow, and held his mouth in a little circle of surprise. "But that's nothing compared to traveling cross-country. I'm amazed, son. You walked all that way cross-country to go to school?"

"Yes, sir. Three times with my uncle, and the last time by myself."

"By yourself? Indeed? Well," said Jackson, leaning back from the table, "I guess if those sorry gold miners can do it, a young Indian boy ought to be able to make the trip."

"But can I come with you?" pressed Adam.

26

The doctor studied Adam for a few moments. "Why not?" he said, clapping his hands and then rubbing them together. "Be on the *Bear* when she sails this morning. You'll take care of that, won't you, Mr. Kelly? Ah-ha, and here's Captain Healy now. Captain, I think you're going to have another passenger if you can find him a berth. Is that all right with you?"

The captain slung one leg over the bench, straddling it as he sat down. The hint of a smile tugged at the corners of his eyes as he sipped his steaming coffee in silence.

In the past, Adam had gone out in the bay on small fishing boats and large "war" canoes, but he had never been to sea in a real ship. And the *Bear* was a real ship, a three-masted cutter with a steam engine that could give it enough speed to catch whiskey smugglers and seal poachers, and enough power to break through ice. It was 198 feet long and 30 feet wide, and it had rescued over five hundred shipwrecked whalers and destitute sailors in the last twelve years.

Each season as it sailed north, it provided the only police protection and medical help for thousands of Eskimos living in villages along the coast of Alaska. But the *Bear* also carried Dr. Sheldon Jackson, Presbyterian missionary and General Agent of Education for the United States Bureau of Education. This remarkable cooperation between Christian missions and the U.S. Government made it possible to establish schools in Alaska long before they could have been supported locally. The government put up most of the money, and the mission boards provided dedicated teachers to run the schools.

A couple days out into the gulf, Adam realized he hadn't seen the missionary for the last twenty-four hours. Seeing Captain Healy standing at the ship's railing by himself, he asked, "Where's Dr. Jackson?"

Captain Healy smiled grimly. "In his cabin, trying to keep from puking his guts out. Don't know how the man does it. He's okay when we're sailing up the inland waterways from Seattle to Sitka, but when we head across the Gulf of Alaska to the Island of Unalaska he always gets sick, and I don't mean a little woozy. He vomits until he's green. But every year he comes back for more. A glutton for punishment, if you ask me."

The bright afternoon sun hung in a silvery sky, sending sheets of glare off the rolling sea. The *Bear*, plunging through swells like a breaching whale crashing back into the water, kicked up a cold, salty spray that stung their faces and took away their breath with its chill.

"You don't like Dr. Jackson very much, do you?" said Adam.

"Of course I like him," Captain Healy growled, staring out toward the distant horizon. "It's just that... he's always pushing his harebrained ideas, and there're some things he ought to leave alone." He ended his sentence on a tone that suggested he had more to say, but he didn't speak. Again Adam caught a whiff of whiskey on his breath.

Curious, Adam pushed a little. "I don't understand. What should he leave alone?"

"Humph. For one thing, he's always trying to get me to become a Christian—his kind of Christian. Oh, I believe in God, all right, but that isn't good enough for him. He wants me to... to change my whole way of living, quit my drinkin' and become like him."

Adam remained silent, but suddenly he remembered a conversation he'd overheard the day they set sail out of Sitka between some of the crew and the new ship's doctor as he'd been exploring the ship.

"He's in his cabin, probably getting drunk again," one of the crew snorted in disgust.

"I think we ought to take over the ship and go back to Sitka," said another sailor in a slow southern drawl. "There's a judge there who'd lock him up for sure. It just ain't right, us white men takin' orders from a slave."

"Former slave," the ship's doctor corrected. "Still don't seem right, though. But that judge in Sitka has no say over maritime matters. We could be charged with mutiny if we're not careful. I suggest we wait until we return to San Francisco and then get him court-martialed for his drinkin'."

"But," the first crewman complained, "what if we get caught in some ice flow and never get back to civilization?"

The conversation had bewildered Adam. Former slave? Captain Healy didn't really look like the African slaves he'd studied about in school—the ones who had been freed by the Emancipation Proclamation more than thirty years earlier. He also remembered the comment the captain had made during Adam's interview about Dr. Jackson trying to get him to stop drinking. But he hadn't seen the captain drunk—except a couple of times during the night, Adam had been awakened by a lot of yelling. And now he again could smell alcohol on the captain's breath.

As they stood together on the plunging deck of the *Bear*, Adam said, "But, Captain Healy, I don't understand. Everyone says you're the best at stopping whiskey smugglers, so why don't you quit drinking yourself?" He knew he shouldn't have said it the moment the words came out of his mouth, but for some reason there was no stopping them. He liked this burly man, and if the captain was in danger of getting court-martialed for his drinking, why didn't he change?

The captain looked coldly out at the sea. "I stop those whiskey smugglers," he said through gritted teeth, the muscles in his jaws bulging as he spoke. "There ain't no one better at enforcing the law. But what I do with myself is my own business—" He turned a dark frown on Adam. "And it ain't none of yours!"

With that, he wheeled and walked away, leaving Adam standing on the deck like an abandoned puppy.

Chapter 3

The Ghost Village

SLEET DROVE STRAIGHT ACROSS the bow of the *Bear* as she plowed through the waves toward St. Lawrence Island late in the afternoon of June 21. Captain Healy had ordered all sails lowered as they neared the island, and the ship was proceeding under steam power. Finally the captain found shelter for his ship in a bay on the leeward side of the Island as a lavender twilight descended over the "land of the midnight sun." Only a couple hundred miles farther north at the Arctic Circle the sun wouldn't set at all that night, just as it would not rise at all on December 21.

Several hours later Adam came on deck after a good sleep in his hammock to find the morning surprisingly calm. A belt of clouds still hung around the mountains on the island, causing their snowy peaks to appear to float in the sky above. Otherwise, the day was clear and beautiful.

"Say, Adam," called the captain, "come on over here." It was the first time he had spoken to Adam since the day he had told the boy to mind his own business. "Uh... I wanna say I'm sorry," mumbled the captain, looking around as though he were making sure no one else heard him. "There was no call for me getting so upset with you the other day." He nodded his head, encouraging Adam to accept his apology.

Adam, not used to anyone asking his forgiveness, looked down, scuffed his right boot on the deck, and finally managed to say, "Yes, sir. I wasn't holdin' a grudge." That was the truth. He had simply been confused by the captain's remarks and had decided to keep his distance.

"Dr. Jackson will probably be in his bunk a couple more hours trying to sleep off the effects of that storm," said the captain. "So he won't notice if we don't lift anchor for a while. What do you say we go ashore? There's something I want to show you."

"Yes, sir," said Adam with a grin.

In moments the captain had two sailors cranking the winch that lowered one of the ship's boats to the water. They all climbed down the rope ladder and were soon bobbing through the choppy water of the bay toward shore.

The island was a stark and barren place compared

to Adam's inland home or the lush forests surrounding Sitka. Low arctic tundra covered the island's rolling knolls near the sea with occasional tufts of taller willows here and there. Most hillsides seemed to be scraped clean of all vegetation, exposing their stony backbones amid crumbling rock slides. The shaded ravines on even the lowest mountains still cradled patches of snow. On the higher mountains, they broadened into glaciers. Only in the seaside meadows did green grass appear.

When the boat crunched to a halt on the pebbly beach, Adam jumped out, eager to feel firm earth under his feet again. But to his astonishment, the ground seemed to sway and move more than the deck of the *Bear*. The sensation was so strong that he stumbled and had to put his hands out for fear of falling.

The sailors roared with laughter. "Can't shake your sea legs, huh, kid?" one of them said, pushing his cap back on his head and sitting on the gunwale of the rowboat.

The captain frowned at them.

"Sorry, sir," the sailor added. Then addressing Adam, he said, "Don't worry; you'll be gettin' your balance in a few steps."

Adam tried again and was finally able to walk in a straight line. "I thought we were having an earthquake," he said as he and the captain trudged up the beach.

The sailors, having stayed behind with the boat, could be heard chuckling to one another.

"How come the ground felt like it was moving?" asked Adam when they were out of earshot.

"It's all in the mind," said Captain Healy. "One gets so used to feeling the movement of the deck that the mind expects it to continue. When it's not there, you imagine it anyway."

Ahead, Adam could see the tops of a few houses above the sand dunes. This would be interesting; an island village. But... something didn't seem quite right. Then he noticed that there were no canoes pulled up on shore, no dogs announced their arrival, and no children ran to meet them.

When they made their way around the dunes and entered the village, Adam could see that it was much larger than he had thought from the few rooftops he had seen from the beach. But most of the buildings were in ruins with their roofs collapsed, and bleached and twisted boards hung askew on crumbling frames like scraps of skin on the old bones of an animal's carcass. Only the occasional house originally built of logs appeared livable. But on an island this far north, logs were rare and came primarily from driftwood washed up on the beach.

Adam approached the first log hut that seemed at least partially intact. Cautiously peeking into the gloom, he said softly, "Hello. Is anyone here?"

A vicious snarl greeted him as a creature lunged toward him out of the darkness. Adam leaped back, tripped on a broken rum keg, and tumbled to the ground. A dark, furry beast rocketed past him and headed into the bushes at the edge of the village.

"A... a wolf," Adam stammered when he got his breath, but the captain was not by his side.

Captain Healy stood thirty feet away where he had stopped at the edge of the grass. "Yep. Probably hiding some food in there or maybe making a den of it for himself," the captain said casually.

Adam picked up a nearby whiskey bottle as he stood to his feet and flung it into the bushes where the wolf had disappeared. "Where are the people?" he asked, knowing that wolves naturally avoided places where people lived.

"Ah. That was a mystery to all of us," said Captain Healy, "but finally we figured it out from the clues. Think you can do the same?"

Adam looked around the village. It was obviously large, probably home for a hundred or more people. But now there wasn't a soul to be seen.

Adam set out with the challenge the captain had given him, searching from house to house. He found rotten kayaks still tied under the eaves of some of the roofs and two huge whalebone boats with their skin covers gnawed off by small animals. The charred ends of small logs that had once been cozy fires and a few hunting spears were propped in the corners of some houses. In the sand around the buildings green, brown, and sometimes lavender whiskey bottles seemed to be everywhere—some whole, some broken.

When Adam came out of one tumbled-down hut, Captain Healy was again waiting for him. "Maybe everyone moved. Maybe they migrated," Adam suggested. "My people often move to keep up with the caribou herds. We always—" He stopped, realizing that he was using the word "we." It wasn't "we" anymore. He was going to make a new life for himself.

The captain looked steadily at him. "But do your people build houses like *this*?"

"No. It would take too much time. Our houses... I mean Tananan houses are made of skins and poles so they can be moved easily."

"Good point," said the captain. "As broken down as these houses look today, they were intended to be permanent. People who build houses like these don't just up and move."

"You're right. And even if they did," said Adam, his eyes shining with the puzzle, "why didn't they take their kayaks and boats and spears? Certainly they would need those things at a new location." He turned to do more investigating.

"I'll give you a hint," the captain said, following after him. "This place has been a ghost village for nearly ten years. When it was first found like this, everyone in it—and I mean everyone—was dead."

Adam stopped and whirled around.

"Of course," continued the captain, "their bodies were later burned, so you don't see their bones lying around now. But otherwise everything looks pretty much the same. So what do you make of that?"

"Everyone died?" Adam felt sick at the thought of all those bodies. He looked at the ground, wondering whether he might be standing on the very place

where a dead body had started to decompose.

"Yes," said the captain solemnly. "Not only in this village but in the next two villages along the coast, every single person was dead!"

"They must have died of some disease," said Adam in shock. He kicked a bottle in disgust. Such uncontrollable sickness was uncommon in the cold north, but in school Adam had learned that plagues had sometimes struck whole civilizations. Still, a few usually survived to tell the story.

"Disease," said the captain, smile lines appearing at the corners of his green eyes. "Yes, I suppose you might call it a disease. But let me give you one more clue. There were no stacks of furs, no pieces of carved ivory, no whalebone, nothing of any value for trading. Other than the bodies and houses in better repair,

things were pretty much as you see them now."

"Maybe all their valuables were stolen," suggested Adam.

"No doubt, but how? When? There was no evidence of a struggle, no signs that the village had been looted after their deaths."

In a daze, Adam walked away. Healy called after him. "The tracks of that disease—if that's what you want to call it—are all around you."

Adam froze and looked around as though he were walking on thin ice. He imagined all those deadly little germs that the French scientist Louis Pasteur had discovered. But they were supposed to be too small to see. All Adam saw were the glittering remnants of broken bottles, half-blackened stones that had once made up fire pits, and boards and other debris that had fallen off the houses.

Broken bottles... that was it! "They drank themselves to death!" he shouted with sudden recognition.

Captain Healy nodded with a grim smile. "But why and how is the sad story." He motioned Adam to follow him over to a large crescent-shaped log that had been dragged into the center of the village long ago. In the center was the remains of an old fire pit. All the bark had been stripped from the log, and it had been worn smooth by the countless Eskimos who had sat around the fire telling stories, reporting on successful whale hunts, and carving ivory.

"For years," began Captain Healy, "poachers have come into these waters from Russia, the United States, England, and Japan to kill the whales and seals and catch the fish that the Eskimos rely on for food, shelter, fuel, and clothing. As a result, it has become harder and harder for the Eskimos to make a living. It has been one of my jobs to stop this poaching, and I have tried.

"But worse than the poaching is the whiskey smuggling. When these robbers could not get enough skins and ivory themselves, they traded whiskey to the Eskimos for their treasures.

"The problem was that in these villages the people had no experience with alcohol. They drank all that the smugglers would give them, and they traded everything of value for more. Their drunken binge lasted for weeks, right through the season when they should have been hunting and fishing for the next winter's food.

"This occurred in each of the three villages that I mentioned. In all, some four hundred men, women, and children died—of starvation. They had not prepared themselves for winter."

"But... didn't any of them escape?" asked Adam.

"Yes, a few made their way through the ice and snow to a fourth village on the far side of the island. In it there was no death. People were not living in ease because there were so few whales, walrus, and seals to be hunted, but at least they were not dying.

"You see," the captain continued, wagging his dark, weathered finger to make his point, "the crooked traders ran out of whiskey and rum before they reached that fourth village. In that village there had been no drunkenness, and the people had secured what food they needed for the winter."

The captain fell silent, and Adam sat there thinking about the tragedy. The image that came to his mind was of himself as a small child about four years old. All the village men were out hunting, and his mother had gotten terribly sick and could not cook. Adam had nothing to eat. Large flakes were falling as he trudged through snow to a neighboring hut where he had begged for some food.

His neighbor had quickly taken him in and given him soup, then went immediately to nurse his mother. But there had been a moment when Adam had stood outside the hut afraid to ask for help, feeling totally alone as a fearful idea had taken shape in his mind: *What if nobody will feed me?*

It was one of those frightening memories from early childhood that are more feeling than fact—indeed, maybe it had only been a dream. Adam couldn't be sure now, but the feeling was real enough as he thought about all the little children in the three villages who had probably gone from house to house begging for food, fighting over the last few scraps they had found.

Out of his swirl of thoughts, Adam blurted, "You work so hard against whiskey smuggling. Why do you—?" He stopped suddenly.

"Go ahead, ask your question," said the captain. "I won't get angry at you."

"No, that's all right," muttered Adam, tossing a pebble into the pit where a thousand fires had burned.

"You were going to ask," the captain said, "since I know how much damage alcohol can do, why do I still drink? And that's exactly why I brought you here. You see, these native people have never had any experience with wine or beer, let alone the hard stuff. They don't know how to manage it, so it consumes and destroys them. They deserve to be protected from it, and especially from those scoundrels who use it to take advantage of them.

"That's different than an educated man like myself who knows what he's doing. Nothing terrible is going to happen just because I take a nip now and then."

"But the sailors said—" Adam stopped again.

The captain cocked an eyebrow. "Yes? What were you going to say?"

Chapter 4

Reindeer Station

ADAM SQUIRMED AS HE SAT on the log in the abandoned village. How had he gotten himself into this? Why couldn't he simply keep his mouth shut?

The captain saw his hesitation. "Look, I'm not going to be angry with you like I was the other day. I'm sorry about that. But if there's something about the crew that I should know, you need to tell me. I'm the captain."

"I know." Adam hesitated, then finally said, "It's the sailors. They're upset about your drinking. They're planning to court-martial you as soon as you get back to San Francisco. Maybe your drinking *is* hurting you more than you realize."

"What do you mean? How do you know this?" Healy leaned forward, clinching his huge fists on his knees.

"I overheard some of them talking," continued Adam. "They don't like you being drunk... but it probably doesn't mean anything," he added as he saw a storm cloud darken the captain's face.

The man's voice became gruff. "You gotta tell me now, son. Every word of it. It's important. I gotta know these things."

"Well," Adam began, struggling to find new courage, "it was the day we left Sitka. One of the crew members was complaining about you being drunk in your cabin again."

"I wasn't drunk!" snapped Healy, shaking his head. "But go ahead; then what happened?"

"This other sailor, the one who talks real slow, he said they ought to take over the ship and go back to Sitka and turn you over to a judge. He said something about white men shouldn't have to take orders from a... from a slave. Then the doctor said that might be considered mutiny and they should wait until they arrived back in San Francisco and court-martial you there."

Captain Healy slumped forward. Planting his elbows on his knees, he massaged his bronzed forehead and thick eyebrows with the tips of his fingers as though he were trying to rub away a headache.

"Captain Healy? What'd they mean about not taking orders from a slave?" asked Adam.

The captain looked at Adam out of the corner of

his eye without taking his head out of his hands. Finally he said, "Yes, you should know." He sat up straight, looking directly at Adam.

"My father was a white plantation owner near Macon, Georgia. My mother was a black woman, his slave. They lived together as husband and wife, but my father was afraid that if he should die, we children—there were ten of us—would be considered slaves. So when each of us got turned ten years old, he sent us north to live and be educated in freedom.

"We all cried when our turn came, but it was a wise choice. Both of my parents died when I was eleven. And that was thirteen years before Lincoln issued the Emancipation Proclamation, let alone the end of the Civil War, so I'd have spent considerable time as a slave if my father hadn't sent me north.

"But my parents' deaths were so upsetting to me that I didn't get much out of my education. I ran away from three schools, and then went to sea at age sixteen. However, by twenty-four, I had settled down and became an officer."

"But you don't look like a Negro," said Adam, searching the captain's green eyes.

A wry smile tugged at the corner of the captain's mouth. "My mother was very light skinned. But in the South, some say it takes only one drop of Negro blood to be considered black. I'm telling you all this, Adam, because I want you to know that I understand what it's like trying to make it in a white man's world. You got some things to learn. First of all, it's a big mistake to turn your back on your own people.

They need you, and you need them. Second, it's all right to be grateful for your education and the kind people who help you, but don't worship white culture or any culture. Choose the good and reject the bad."

The captain nodded his head, signifying the end of his speech, then got up and stretched like he was very tired and his bones ached. "Let's get back to the ship."

That afternoon the *Bear* made its way around St. Lawrence Island to the village of Gambell. This time it was Dr. Jackson who invited Adam to go ashore. There were nineteen mission stations in Alaska, with a total of sixty-one missionaries, and the one at Gambell was the farthest west. Eight others were in Eskimo villages on the Bering Sea. Three were far to the north along the coast of the Arctic Ocean. And seven were in the valley of the Yukon River.

As Dr. Jackson and Adam walked up the beach

to the mission school, people came running from all directions, beaming happily and talking excitedly in their native language. Some of the mothers held up new babies; men beckoned Dr. Jackson as if wanting him to follow them. "They want to show off their reindeer herds," Jackson told Adam, nodding greetings first to one, then another. Soon the local missionary arrived and helped interpret.

When they had followed several of the young men out to the reindeer corrals, Dr. Jackson stopped and swept his arm toward the reindeer. Corrals full of antlered beasts filled half the horizon. "Look at that," he said with satisfaction. "Even if these people had a terrible season hunting and fishing, they wouldn't starve."

Then he turned directly to Adam. "I understand Captain Healy showed you that empty village this morning."

Adam nodded, recalling the ghost village.

"When I heard what had happened in those villages," the missionary explained to his young com-

panion, "I decided we had to do something. Captain Healy does his best to keep out poachers and whiskey smugglers, but we couldn't wait around for the whales and walrus and seals to come back so these people would have enough to eat.

"I had seen how the Siberians, not fifty miles west across the Bering sea, raised reindeer for food and beasts of burden. Those deer can be taught how to pull sleds and carry packs, you know. Anyway, I said to myself, 'Why not bring some over for the Eskimos to raise?' Captain Healy was all for it, so that's what we did. Now just look."

Then with a chuckle he added, "If you think that's a big herd, wait until you see the herds at the Teller Station. That's a real enterprise."

Enterprise, thought Adam. *That must be the key to Dr. Jackson's success. That must be the way to "make it in a white man's world," as Captain Healy put it.* He decided he would look for a way to be enterprising.

The *Bear* departed early the next morning, sailing northeast all day and reaching Nome on the mainland before sunset that night. The next three days were spent going from port to port up the coast, visiting various Eskimo villages until the *Bear* finally dropped anchor late on Saturday, June 26, in Port Clarence Bay.

Because the ship carried so many supplies for the mission and Teller Reindeer Station—lumber and heavy barrels of tools, food stuffs, and bolts of cloth—Captain Healy launched the ship's steam-powered launch early the next morning. But, since it was Sunday, he did not begin off-loading the cargo. Instead, Adam, Dr. Jackson, Captain Healy, and several of the crew went ashore just in time to attend Sunday worship services in the recently built little schoolhouse.

A strange mix of people crowded into the rough, unpainted building. The majority were Eskimos from the village of Nook across Port Clarence Bay. Adam wondered if their effort to come across the bay by boat meant that they were responding to the Gospel or if they'd seen the *Bear* arrive the night before and simply wanted to see the visitors.

Also in attendance were several red-faced, blond-haired families in the most unusual costumes. The men wore brightly colored short jackets with yellow, red, and blue trim—much of it embroidery. The women also wore brightly colored clothes along with high-topped, brimless, red hats with flaps that tied under their chins. These, too, were decorated with embroidery.

Seeing Adam's curious stares, Dr. Jackson whispered, "Those are Lapps, families from Lapland who came here to teach the Eskimos how to herd the reindeer. That man over there"—he pointed to a white man with heavy facial features and a full black beard—"is William Kjellmann. He's the superintendent of this station. He's a Lapp, too, but he lived for several years in Madison, Wisconsin, before I brought him to Alaska. He's the one who got these other families to come over here from Norway."

While Dr. Jackson had been speaking, Superintendent Kjellmann had been making his way through the small crowd to greet Dr. Jackson and Captain Healy. As they entered the building, Dr. Jackson said, "Oh, Kjellmann, this is Adam Christian, a Tananan boy who's traveling with me."

Adam shook the man's hand as they went in.

Rev. Tollef Brevig, a Lutheran minister from Lapland who had lived in the United States for some time before coming to Alaska, led the services in the Eskimo language. The room was packed, every bench filled, and around three sides men stood leaning against the rough-sawed boards of the walls, while women and children stood in front of them.

Even with the windows open, the smell of so many people in such a small room was like a barrel full of smoked fish. But they sang eagerly and loudly, the high-pitched voices of the women sliding from note to note with a nose-pinched twang, while the lower tones of the men did not always make it to the right notes.

Dr. Jackson was asked to give the sermon, which Rev. Brevig translated to the eager audience.

Adam's mind began to wander. Maybe he should have gone to Skagway and hauled freight up over the Chilkoot Pass for those miners. With the money he could have made, he might have started some "enterprise" when he reached the States. This trip with Dr. Jackson was beginning to feel like a waste of time.

After the service, Dr. Jackson stood at the door as

everyone streamed past, shaking his hand vigorously and speaking a few words in English if they could—most being either Eskimos or from Lapland.

While they ate their noon meal at the Kjellmann house, Dr. Jackson explained that he had been commissioned by the secretary of agriculture to explore the land along the Yukon with the possibility of encouraging settlement.

"Do you think you could come with me, Bill?" Jackson asked. "I need someone who understands reindeer and knows exactly what they need to eat."

Kjellmann's rugged face screwed up into a frown as he slid the food on his plate from side to side. He glanced toward his wife, and Adam noticed that she gave him a quick frown. "I don't know, Dr. Jackson," he said in his thick Scandinavian accent. "Dis is an awfully busy season. We're running close to 450 deer in our herd, ya know, and we got to keep dem moving so dey don't overgraze. Besides, I got to take me a long trip this fall when I take back some of dem Lapps to Norvay, de ones who have finished dier time here and don't want to stay. I don't vant to be avay from home too long." He smiled at his wife.

"We'll be back long before that," said Jackson. "I need you, Bill. And if you're worried about overgrazing around here, maybe we could move part of your herd up there... if we find a good location."

"My herd? But why my herd? I t'ought you were looking for agricultural possibilities. What's all dis talk about reindeer?"

"Because..." Jackson paused and then wagged

his finger at Kjellmann. "You've heard about the gold strike up along Bonanza Creek in the Klondike region of Canada last year, didn't you?"

"Yah, I heard talk, but somebody's always finding a little flake here and dere—along Forty Mile River, Franklin Gulch, Troublesome Point. It's been happening for years. Dis is Alaska, ya know. It don't mean much."

"Ah, but I think it does. This was more than a few sparkles in the bottom of some old-timer's pan. It was a real strike, and miners are starting to pour into the region. I've heard that every boat going up the Yukon is full of 'em. If they start pulling large amounts of gold out of there, there'll be thousands of people racing up here from the States. You mark my words."

Adam noticed how Dr. Jackson was always thinking ahead, always looking for the opportunity for enterprise. He thought again of the miners climbing the pass out of Skagway.

"Some are taking the overland route," added Adam. Both men turned to look at him, somewhat surprised at his entering their conversation. Adam felt embarrassed and searched for something to say that would show that he knew what he was talking about. "They're climbing the Chilkoot Pass out of Skagway. We heard about it all the time down at Sitka. They go through Whitehorse, following the headwaters of the Yukon until they get to Dawson. I know that country. That's close to the route I took coming to school."

"Yes, the Chilkoot Pass," said Dr. Jackson. "See, Bill, even this boy knows about 'em. I tell you; it could turn into a real gold rush." Dr. Jackson stopped to shovel some beans into his mouth. Then he looked up expectantly at Kjellmann.

"So?" said the superintendent. "Vhat's dat have to do wit' *my* reindeer?"

"Don't you see? It would be like California in '49. They'll be needing supplies, mail deliveries, food... and they'll pay good money for it, too."

Adam looked back and forth between the two men. He could see Dr. Jackson's point, so why was Kjellmann staring so blankly at Jackson?

"Look," said Dr. Jackson, "we've been having trouble getting enough money either from the government or from private sources to bring more reindeer over here. So far we've helped the local Eskimos avoid starvation, but we didn't bring any new deer over from Siberia last year or this year, and the furs and ivory and whalebone the Eskimos are able to trade don't begin to pay for transporting more deer. But if we could employ several teams of reindeer in providing transportation along the Yukon in the winter, that could bring in some much-needed hard cash. If we can get those routes set up before there's a real stampede of gold miners into the area, we'll be sitting pretty."

Yes! thought Adam with a surge of excitement. He understood what Dr. Jackson was talking about. He was able to think like him. Maybe he would also become a success like him.

53

Kjellmann looked at Dr. Jackson for several moments and finally said, "So you vant me to go wit' you up the Yukon to find a place where you can send some of my best teams just so you can get year-round mail to a bunch of old sourdough prospectors? Humph. Let 'em use dog sleds."

"But don't you see?" said Dr. Jackson. "This would show the rest of the world that reindeer are profitable, that we're not running an endless charity program here. And it might raise enough money for you to get even more deer."

Kjellmann's frown returned. "Who'd take care of dem?" he asked.

"I don't know. There's a good mission up there—St. James. It's where this boy comes from," Jackson said, nodding toward Adam. "Maybe his people would be interested in becoming herders."

"Not very likely," said Kjellmann. "Dose Tananan are nomadic hunters. I doubt you could get dem to stay in one place long enough to care for a herd."

"That's exactly what you said about the Eskimos! Give 'em a chance."

Kjellmann pursed his lips in a long moment of silence. "Oh, all right; I go," grumped Kjellmann, glancing at his wife to see how disapproving she might be. She only shrugged. "Vhen you plan to leave?" he asked.

Chapter 5

"Gold! Gold! Gold!"

GOLDEN CLOUDS RIBBED the blue northeastern sky like loosely twisted ropes of cotton, announcing sunrise to the sleepy town of St. Michael, Alaska. But no one awoke. It was only two o'clock in the morning.

Two hours later, what did rouse the merchants, saloon keepers, dance hall girls, dock workers and fishermen, whalers and sailors, Eskimos and Indians, restaurant cooks and boarding house matrons, and everyone sleeping on the two ships anchored off shore was the urgent hooting of the whistle on the Yukon River steamboat, the *Portus B. Ware*, as it came chugging around

Whale Island and headed toward St. Michael.

In its path were anchored the *Bear* and the *Portland*, which had recently arrived from Seattle. The water of Norton Sound was calm, and the two ships were not far apart, but the little riverboat seemed to be puffing right toward them.

This was as far as the *Bear* was taking Dr. Jackson, Mr. Kjellmann, and Adam, who were spending one last night on board.

"What's going on?" cried Adam as he scrambled up on deck to stand along the railing with several sailors and Captain Healy. Many of the men weren't fully dressed yet and hopped around on the cold deck as they pulled on boots or shrugged into shirts and snapped their suspenders over their shoulders.

Black smoke billowed out of the smokestack of the little steamer. "They must be having trouble with their boiler and are afraid it's going to blow," said one of the sailors, referring to all the smoke and whistle blowing.

"That better not be the case," growled Captain Healy. "They're getting much too close for comfort." He began waving his arms to direct the little riverboat away.

Instead, it chugged straight ahead, and those on board the *Bear* could see that, while it wasn't on a direct collision course with either the *Bear* or the *Portland*, it was headed right between them. A very dangerous maneuver. On deck of the little steamer stood the passengers waving their arms and shouting.

"If that thing blows, we're all done for," muttered

an anxious Captain Healy.

"Maybe it's comin' 'long side," said Mr. Kjellmann as he came up behind Adam.

"Not at that speed," the captain said darkly.

The *Portus B. Ware* did not cut its speed. It chugged and hooted right between the two larger ships. As it did so, everyone on deck of both ships heard what the riverboat passengers were shouting.

"Gold! Gold! Gold!"

"We got piles of the yellow stuff! Everyone's rich!"

"It's a huge strike!"

Once it had cleared the larger ships, the riverboat slowed and prepared to dock at the little wharf built out from the town of St. Michael.

Adam looked at Captain Healy. Knots were bulging the captain's cheeks as he mumbled through clinched teeth, "Gold or not, that fool pilot had no business endangering my ship."

But Adam was curious about the excited miners on the riverboat. He'd always shrugged off a miner's life as hard work with little reward. But if there really was gold, *lots* of gold, right here in Alaska .... His thoughts tumbled. Maybe becoming a gold miner was a way to make a success of himself, right here in his own country.

By the time Adam, Dr. Jackson, and Mr. Kjellmann managed to find space in the *Bear*'s longboat and make their way to shore, everyone in town was awake and celebrating. Some were shooting their guns in the air. Others were drinking—even though it was early morning—and people were running from one person to another telling one another again what everyone had already heard. Gold! There had been a big strike in the Klondike.

The vague reports of gold discovered along Rabbit Creek the summer before had seemed like nothing at the time. But the prospectors who had been smart enough to follow the first rumors had found their fortunes; today everyone in town was calling it "Bonanza Creek." The reckless little riverboat had brought back sixty-eight men who decided to cash in what they'd already collected, and soon the news was all over town: they'd brought in over half a million dollars worth of gold and word that the biggest strikes were yet to come.

A grizzled old-timer with a huge yellowed beard limped down the boardwalk toward Adam, Dr. Jackson, and Mr. Kjellmann. Over his left shoulder he carried a worn-out shovel and a broken pick. He grinned, exposing a mouth with very few teeth as he held up a small but obviously heavy sack in his right hand. "I'm cashin' this in. Then I'm gettin' resupplied and headin' right back up there," he said with a nod of his head.

Adam stood watching as the man hobbled on down the street.

"See what I told you?" said Jackson to Kjellmann. "Now's the time to get the reindeer in place. Those miners will be crying for supplies and transportation before winter." Jackson was speaking the obvious. Though riverboats like the *Portus B. Ware* did a swift business during summer, by mid-September

58

ice would form again and block river travel. And that ice would not break up until late May or June.

"Adam," said Dr. Jackson, "here's some money. I want you to go right now and book passage for all three of us on the *Portus B. Ware* to Dawson. If we wait any longer, there won't be room. Kjellmann, come with me. We need to send a message back to the secretary of agriculture about what's happening. This is going to change Alaska forever!"

Adam headed for the waterfront and was surprised to find a line of people already standing on the wharf waiting to buy passage on the *Portus B. Ware* when it headed back up the Yukon. Among them were four sailors with nothing but their sea bags slung over their shoulders. They looked around furtively and kept low behind other people in line as though they didn't want anyone to see them. *They must have jumped ship,* thought Adam, *and don't want to get caught.* But he didn't recognize them, so he figured they must have come from the *Portland.*

Both men and women stood in line, probably residents of St. Michael who were off to find greener—or in this case, more golden—pastures. A few carried a pick and a shovel and a large pack, but other than that, no one had any mining equipment that Adam could see. *Maybe they don't need any heavy equipment,* he thought. He imagined the shiny nuggets sitting on the surface of the ground like buttercups in the spring.

"You planning on gettin' rich?" said a familiar voice behind him.

Adam jumped. Turning, he found Captain Healy surveying the line of hopefuls wanting passage on the *Portus B. Ware.*

"You startled me!" Adam admitted. He felt his face flush. Did the captain know what he was thinking? "W-what are you doing here?" he stammered, trying to change the subject.

"Oh, just makin' sure none of my boys caught this gold fever," the captain said dryly, his eyes moving up and down the line along the wharf. "But I might ask you the same question. Changing your mind about going to the States, are you?"

"Oh no, sir! Dr. Jackson sent me to buy tickets to Dawson. Good thing I came when I did, though. Pretty soon there might not be any space left."

The captain nodded and, having satisfied himself that none of his sailors were in line, looked for the first time directly at Adam. "You think there's any gold in those creeks and streams you fished in as a little boy?" he asked.

Adam shrugged. He'd never paid any attention.

"Well, be careful. Gold fever's a powerful bug to be bit by. I've seen men turn their hands into bloody stumps clawin' through the gravel in an old stream. The freezing water numbed 'em so that they didn't even feel the pain."

Adam looked out over Norton Sound where a light breeze had kicked up ripples that glistened like gold flakes. "I'll be okay," he said stubbornly.

"Well, good luck to you, son," said the captain, holding out his hand. "I hope you find what you're looking for. But you remember what I said: whatever you do, don't forget your own people. They need everything you've learned in school... or ever will learn. That's real success!"

Adam wished the captain would quit lecturing him. Still, as he shook the captain's hand, he wasn't eager to say good-bye. "Won't I see you again?" he asked.

"Maybe, maybe not." The captain shrugged. "It all depends on where the *Bear* is when you and the doctor get back from Dawson. If another ship is here and headed back to Seattle, he'll probably take it."

Adam watched as the captain walked away, then suddenly realized that the line for tickets on the *Portus B. Ware* had shuffled forward.

After purchasing the tickets, Adam had five dollars left over. On his way to find Dr. Jackson and Mr. Kjellmann, he met the same toothless prospector they had passed earlier on the boardwalk. However, this time the old man wasn't grinning, and he didn't carry his bag of gold. Instead, he was using his worn-out D-handled spade like a cane. His other hand hung at his side with a half-empty bottle of whiskey dangling from it.

"Hey, sonny," he mumbled, his words slurring together, "ya wanna buy a shovel? Los' m' grubstake an' need somethin' ta eat."

Adam looked up and down the boardwalk. Lots of people were still out on the street, but he didn't see anyone he knew. He thought of what Captain Healy had said about men using their bare hands to dig for

gold. It sure wouldn't hurt to have a shovel along if he had a chance to do a little prospecting. He didn't want to be digging with his hands.

"How much?" he asked quickly.

"How much ya got?"

Adam pulled out the five-dollar bill and held it close to his chest with both hands as he considered what he should do. The money wasn't really his, but then Dr. Jackson wouldn't know the price of the tickets. On a sold-out trip, tickets might cost any amount.

Then, quick as a rabbit, the old man grabbed the five dollars and said, "Here!" as he dropped the shovel in front of Adam and hobbled off down the street.

Adam stood looking after the old man, confused by his desire to have the shovel and knowing he had no right to spend Dr. Jackson's money without his permission. *But it wasn't my fault the old man took the money,* he tried to assure himself. Still, he knew that he could have caught the old man and at least tried to get the money back. Was it stealing to keep the shovel? How would he explain it? He could just say he found it. That wasn't so bad... or was it?

On July 5, Adam, Dr. Jackson, and Mr. Kjellmann were on the *Portus B. Ware* as it steamed away from the wharf at St. Michael, rounded the point in Norton Sound, and headed toward the Yukon Delta, trying to find a branch of the river it could safely travel.

Whenever the *Portus B. Ware* stopped for wood at places like Russian Mission, Anvik, and Galena, Dr.

Jackson took a little walk on shore to collect soil and plant samples for the secretary of agriculture.

On the afternoon that the rear paddle-wheeler chugged up to the dock at the St. James Mission, Adam was on deck with many of the other passengers, slapping mosquitoes into red and brown blotches of goo on his arms and neck. The St. James Mission and the little village of Tanana were just downriver from where the Tanana River dumped into the Yukon. Adam was entering his homeland. His people spent most of their time up the Tanana River Valley, but they were a migratory tribe, fishing for salmon in the summer and following the caribou herds when they came through in the fall and spring. So they often traveled this far west.

Once the *Portus B. Ware* had docked, and Dr. Jackson and Mr. Kjellmann had disembarked, Adam dug out the shovel that he had sneaked on board and hurried after them. "Dr. Jackson," he called, "look what I have. You can use it to gather your plant samples."

There, Adam thought, *I've said it. If he doesn't ask too many questions about how I came by this shovel, I won't have to explain or hide it anymore. And if he uses it, then it doesn't matter that his money paid for it.*

"Great," said the doctor. "I'm tired of getting my fingernails full of dirt. But I've got to talk to Father Chapman. William," he said, taking the shovel and handing it to Mr. Kjellmann, "would you get some samples from that moss you said looked so good along the bank?"

Adam walked with Dr. Jackson as he went to find Father Chapman, the Episcopal missionary who ran the school at St. James. They found the young missionary chopping wood behind the little log chapel. It was a sturdy building with a log belfry that rose above it on one corner, making it look like the block house of a fort.

"Gnob?" said Father Chapman, recognizing Adam. "My, how you've grown. Why, he's taller than you, Dr. Jackson."

Dr. Jackson coughed with embarrassment, and Adam wisely changed the conversation. "I don't use Gnob anymore, Father Chapman. I am Adam Christian now, and I've just graduated from the Sitka Industrial and Training School. I'm traveling with Dr. Jackson to the States."

"You don't say!" Father Chapman slapped Adam on the shoulder.

"Yes," said Dr. Jackson. "Adam won the prize I was offering. I trust you got my letter announcing the contest, but I never heard back from you with the names of any applicants."

It was Father Chapman's turn to fumble for an answer. "I suppose we didn't have any students the quality of young Gnob... I mean Adam, here. I take my hat off to you, Adam." He briefly lifted his little pillbox of Russian fur.

"But there's something else I want to discuss with you," Jackson hurried on. "Mr. Kjellmann, my expert on reindeer, tells me that the moss growing around here is just the thing reindeer need."

"I suppose so," agreed Father Chapman. "When the caribou come through, they sure seem to like it. But the fact is, we haven't seen very many this year. I think all the miners upriver have spooked 'em away. I don't know what the Indians are going to do come winter. In fact, I'm quite worried this year."

"That's just my point," said Dr. Jackson excitedly. "They'll need food, and reindeer are just the solution. Over on the coast the Eskimos were having trouble because the whale and seal populations were declining, so we brought in the reindeer. Now their villages are stable again, and they're learning to be farmers. Adam, here, has seen it for himself!"

The missionary stroked his beard thoughtfully. "I'm not sure," he said. "These Indians don't stay in one place like farmers. When the salmon are running, they usually camp around here and fish the Yukon and Tanana Rivers, but much of the year they follow the caribou herds."

"Well," said Dr. Jackson, "they would have to move the reindeer herds from time to time to find better pastures, so some migration would be possible once they learned how to care for them. But don't you find your mission work hard if your people are always on the move?"

"That's their way of life," said the missionary. "Who am I to try to change it?"

"Maybe so, maybe not," Jackson persisted. "But even if the Indians aren't interested, reindeer could help make money to run your mission. Even if you just hired some Lapps to manage a herd for you.

"Look, I can get you adult deer at about $7.50 apiece. A fawn during the first four years costs about a dollar a year for upkeep. But then you can sell them for meat at $50 to $100 each. That's a tremendous profit! With all those gold miners coming in, they're gonna need meat. And if you want to train them to the sled or pack, you could be part of a transportation network to the gold field."

"Hmm. I'm not sure I want to run a freight company," said Father Chapman wryly. "I've got my mission work in the school."

Jackson's normally square shoulders sagged in exasperation, and he closed his eyes for a moment as though praying for patience. "All right, all right. But just think about it, Father. It could be important."

Just then the shrill whistle of the *Portus B. Ware* sounded.

"Besides," said Dr. Jackson, as Father Chapman walked them back to the river, "if you really do care about these Indians, this might be just the thing to prevent hunger among them."

They waved at the young missionary as the boat chugged away, its rear paddle wheel splashing with the rhythm of a bass drum in the cold river. "Now, Adam," said Dr. Jackson, turning to the boy, "there's something I want to ask you."

Adam's throat tightened, and he felt a funny tingling down the back of his neck. Would he have to explain the shovel?

67

Chapter 6

Stranded

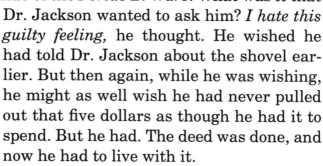

A DAM LOOKED DOWN AT THE WATER churning along the side of the *Portus B. Ware*. What was it that Dr. Jackson wanted to ask him? *I hate this guilty feeling,* he thought. He wished he had told Dr. Jackson about the shovel earlier. But then again, while he was wishing, he might as well wish he had never pulled out that five dollars as though he had it to spend. But he had. The deed was done, and now he had to live with it.

"Since this is your homeland," began Dr. Jackson, "what do you remember about fields of moss? Does this tundra we see along the river extend all the way up the Tanana River Valley?"

"Uh..." Adam was so relieved that the doctor wasn't asking about the shovel that for a few moments he couldn't focus on what Dr. Jackson had asked him. "I... uh... oh yes, the valley, or rather the moss. You want to know about the moss. Yes, yes, all along the valley up the Tanana River, tundra and woods is mostly all there is."

"How about to the north?" Jackson gestured to the port side of the boat. A large moose raised its head from the shallows along the bank. Plants and water streamed from its mouth as it casually chewed and watched the riverboat steam past.

Adam looked at the Ray Mountains that came down almost to the river's edge. "Uh... that's pretty rough country up that way," he said. "But the Kanuti Flats are up there. And if you go all the way to the Endicott Mountains, the trees stop. Then there's nothing but tundra. But I've never been that far."

Sheldon Jackson nodded his head absentmindedly, then turned back toward the south—off the starboard side of the boat—and gazed up the Tanana River Valley as though he were expecting to see herds of reindeer grazing in the clearings between the thick stands of poplar, black spruce, alder, and willow.

Adam watched the missionary, who seemed deep in thought, feeling relieved that he hadn't been caught in his little lie. But maybe... maybe he should just say something and get it off his chest.

Finally he blurted, "Dr. Jackson, there's something I need to tell you." He waited for the man's attention. "Dr. Jackson?"

Hearing the urgency in Adam's voice, Jackson broke the spell of whatever he was dreaming about and said, "Yes, Adam. What is it?"

With Jackson looking him right in the eye, Adam almost lost his nerve, but he swallowed hard and said, "I kind of took something that didn't belong to me."

Jackson frowned. "You stole something?"

"Well, not exactly." Adam's eyes fell to the churning water. "But I got something for it that's not really mine."

"What in the world are you talking about, son?"

"The shovel!" Adam blurted. "The one Mr. Kjellmann used to dig samples back there. It's not really mine!"

"Not yours?" Jackson's voice held a note of irritation. "Make yourself plain, boy."

So Adam told him the whole story from the point of getting excited about looking for gold to the five dollars the old prospector had grabbed out of his hand in exchange for the shovel.

"Humph," said Jackson. "Looks like I bought myself a shovel whether I wanted one or not, doesn't it?"

"Yes, sir." Adam turned away to stare at the passing riverbank, unable to look the doctor in the eye any longer. He expected the man's hawklike expression to burst forth in a scolding at the very least, but Jackson put both hands on the rail and stared at the shore in silence.

Finally Adam couldn't take the quiet any longer. "I'm sorry, sir," he said mournfully.

Dr. Jackson put his hand on Adam's shoulder and

turned him so they again looked each other in the eye. In spite of the teacher's sharp eyes, tiny spectacles, and pointed beard, the irritation was completely gone from his face. "And I forgive you because you owned up to it. However, I want you to understand one thing; it's my shovel. If you want to use it, you must ask me. Is that agreed?"

"Yes, sir." Adam grinned with relief. "Thank you!"

That night Adam came out on the deck by himself to gaze at the star-spangled sky. It was so deep, so crisp and cold, even in summer. To the north he could see ribbons of color flicker into the night like blue flame. They fanned higher and shimmered with red, purple, and green. Gold and silver flashed through them and shot off across the sky. Finally they settled into the images of iridescent curtains hung from the stars that gently folded and waved as though blown by some soft, cosmic breeze.

Would he be able to see the northern lights from the States? Such a show had always filled him with awe. He would miss it down south.

The trip to Dawson City—which was not really a city at all but a fast-growing town at the center of the gold field—was over 1,600 miles from St. Michael and took the *Portus B. Ware* twenty days before it arrived on Friday, July 25. Dawson was actually in Canadian territory, situated on a floodplain just below a great slash of bare rock cut into a hill called

Midnight Dome, just below the point where the Klondike River joined the Yukon.

As the stern-wheeler approached the bend, bell ringing and whistle blowing, it chugged toward the little dock at the river's edge. Dozens of eager prospectors and townspeople welcomed the mail, supplies, and returning friends that the *Portus B. Ware* brought.

All that day Adam had noticed miners working their claims along the bank wherever a small stream poured into the great river. Some rose to wave as the boat steamed past. Others ignored them like an old bear interested only in catching salmon. A few prospectors had taken time to put up a shack or pitch a tent, but many camps were nothing more than a coffeepot hanging over a smoldering fire with a couple bedrolls thrown alongside.

This would be different, though, he thought. This was Dawson City, the heart of the gold rush.

But when Adam stepped off the end of the pier into the disarray of half-finished log cabins and slapped-up stores, he sank in goo halfway up his calf. The second step was no better.

The streets—if you could call them that in a town where people built wherever they wanted to—were a mud pit. The layer of frozen ground a foot or two down that never thawed, even in the warmest summer, was called permafrost, and it prevented water from soaking in. Water that didn't find its way into the river was whipped into a soup by every boot or cart that trudged up the street.

But the busy people of Dawson didn't seem to

mind. Tent saloons, clapboard shacks, half-finished
log buildings, and open campsites sprouted every-

where. And everyone seemed to be in a hurry—after all, there was gold to be found and money to be made.

Dr. Jackson and Mr. Kjellmann hurried off to discover the potential for a reindeer transport company to Dawson while Adam was left to nose around the town. "We're leaving tomorrow, so don't get yourself lost," Jackson said. "But stay away from those women with painted faces. We'll find you later."

Tomorrow! Adam thought. Not much chance he'd get to dig for gold. Disgruntled, he strolled around town gawking at the stores and peeking in the saloons where gambling games were in full swing. Filthy miners were sitting at the tables with their little bags of gold dust or cashing them in for poker chips worth $500 and even $1,000. They were so eager to multiply their fortune that they hadn't even taken time to get a bath. At one table, a fight broke out as a prospector lost his entire poke of gold to a slick gambler.

It didn't take Adam long to figure out who was really getting rich in Dawson. A shirt cost $5, when he could have gotten the same one back in Sitka for fifty cents. A pair of rubber boots was tagged at an incredible $25. Then he saw a little store, nothing more than a row of split logs lying in the mud with a tent over it and a sign that said, "Pans, Picks, and Shovels $15 each." Not one item was new.

Hey, thought Adam, *if I can't use my shovel, might as well sell it, return Dr. Jackson's money, and still have ten bucks left over. That's good enterprise!* He grinned, using a word he'd learned from Dr. Jackson. Racing back to the riverboat, he retrieved the shovel and was soon back at the little "hardware" store.

"Sir, I've got a shovel here I'd like to sell you," said Adam, holding it out. He was a tall, thin fellow wearing an old army jacket and cap. A huge mustache covered his lips and drooped at the ends to his chin. His bushy eyebrows seemed almost as large.

The man took the shovel and examined it at arm's length as though he were inspecting a new rifle. "Believe I've seen this here tool," he drawled in a deep, lazy voice. "Yep! There's my mark." He pointed to a little notch in the handle. "I reckon I sold it to an old sourdough headin' downriver 'bout a month ago."

"That's possible," said Adam. "I bought it in St. Michael from a man who had made his fortune here in the gold fields. So I 'spect it's a pretty lucky shovel."

"Give you five bucks for it," said the storekeeper.

"Five? But you're selling them for $15," said Adam.

"Yeah, but it's been a slow day. Maybe business is droppin' off, and I'll have to lower my prices. Seven's as high as I'll go. I gotta make a livin', too, ya know."

So the deal was closed, and Adam walked away with $7, disgruntled at only making a $2 profit.

That night Sheldon Jackson, William Kjellmann, and Adam slept on board the riverboat. "If you bunked a dog in any of those hotels in Dawson, it'd come out with more lice than it went in with," grumbled Dr. Jackson. "You're not gettin' me to sleep there."

Adam decided now wasn't a good time to give Dr. Jackson his money. He'd do it later.

❖ ❖ ❖ ❖

The next day all three of them were on board the *Portus B. Ware* as it headed back down the Yukon carrying more gold and satisfied fortune seekers. It was a beautiful day to be on the river in such beautiful country. On one of the many islands, Adam saw a black bear pawing in the shallows, halfheartedly fishing for salmon. But the sight of the great animal brought a moment of concern to Adam: This was the only bear he had seen when usually they would have been a common sight along the river. And he had seen only one moose. Where was the wildlife?

He slapped at some mosquitoes, one on his neck and another biting his hand. At least the insect population was still as large as ever.

Two days later the *Portus B. Ware* approached the beginning of the Yukon Flats, a section where the river divided into scores of channels and small streams meandering through hundreds of low islands and ever-shifting sandbars. Swamp stretched out for miles on both sides of the river, making travel along the banks nearly impossible in the summer. In the river, the going was slow as the pilot constantly searched for snags and new sandbars.

As darkness approached, a thick fog arose from the river, which further hampered travel. They should have arrived at Fort Yukon well before dark, but finally the word was sent around that they must have missed it. "But don't be concerned, folks," said the captain. "We have plenty of fuel to make it to Beaver or even Steven's Village if we have to."

With that, Adam curled up to sleep between two stacks of baggage on the deck. One was a stack of empty whiskey barrels, and the other was a pile of personal baggage covered by a large canvas tarpaulin. But about midnight, a loud grating sound woke him. The boat's whistle blew, and the pilot began yelling to reverse the engine, and then there was such a lurch that the stack of barrels toppled over and rolled toward the front of the deck, hitting Adam on the way. Instantly, the boat came to a complete stop, listing about ten degrees to the port side.

There was no question what had happened. They had gone aground on a sandbar.

He could hear the paddle wheel begin its steady *thuff, thuff, thuff* as it reversed direction, attempting to pull the boat free. "Get some lanterns down here!" yelled someone who had run past Adam. He tripped and fell over the empty barrels and came up cursing and throwing them into the river so he could get to the prow of the boat to see how badly it was stuck.

When the lights arrived, Adam could see that only a short distance from the boat the water's depth decreased to no more than a foot. The longer they remained grounded, the more the river's current would drive the boat farther onto the sandbar. The passengers were quickly herded to the back of the boat. "Take your luggage with you!" a deckhand yelled, ripping the tarpaulin off the baggage and throwing it overboard. "We need to lighten the front of this tub if it's going to float free again."

When that didn't work, all able-bodied people

were urged to disembark and stand in the shallows. Everyone except a mother and her two young children and another woman climbed over the railing and huddled together in the icy water on the sandbar. Lanterns hung from the boat railing cast an eerie glow through the fog, and the smokestack glowed red as it spit sparks and smoke into the black night. Adam was a good swimmer, but as he stood up to his waist in the frigid Yukon, with the river current tugging him downstream and the dark bulk of the riverboat looming overhead, he could feel panic rising in his chest.

"Everybody stay together, now," yelled one of the boat hands. "We don't want anybody stepping off into deeper water. The current feels gentle here, but it can grab you mighty quick."

All this while, the steam engine hissed and chugged as the paddle wheel clawed at the river in an attempt to free the prow. Everyone worked for hours, those who could get close enough, putting their shoulder to the boat, trying to push it off the sand.

Finally the pilot called a halt to their efforts and told everyone to get back on board. They'd wait until daylight. Maybe then there would be more hope of getting free. "Besides, we've got to save some of this firewood so we can have power later when we need it." In an attempt to keep up full steam so the paddle wheel could have every chance of pulling them off the sandbar, the crew had fed cordwood into the boiler's firebox at such a rate that the pile of split logs was now frighteningly small.

Chapter 7

The Whiskey Barrel Kayak

MORNING'S LIGHT DID NOT BRING good news. The pilot and the deckhands couldn't recognize where they were. The islands that choke the Yukon along this 250-mile stretch of flat, swampy land were forever changing. There were no reference points in the Flats, no mountain peaks, no bluffs, nothing higher on the horizon than the thick growths of scraggly spruce and dense alder and willow brush that topped the thousands of low, shifting islands amid the meandering streams and branches of the great river.

One might as well be out on the ocean or the Sahara Desert. Were they above or below Fort Yukon? At some time prior to running aground the

79

night before, they must have veered into the wrong channel, one that they now saw was not deep enough for safe passage, even if they could get the boat free.

The only hope was to back it up until they could switch into a deeper channel. Again, time was important because the hull was becoming more and more entrapped as the relentless current pressed it forward while the shifting sand sucked it deeper.

Employing buckets and shovels and anything that could scoop sand, the crew and a few volunteers took turns trying to dig and then push the boat free.

Later, up on deck while he was trying to get warm, Adam tried to figure where they were. He knew this area. In winter, his people often traveled across the frozen waste to trade at Fort Yukon.

Downstream from the stuck riverboat was a low island that apparently began with the sandbar on which the boat was stuck. Caught in the tangle of willows and driftwood along its upstream bank, Adam spied several of the empty barrels and the tarp that had been thrown overboard the night before.

Looking to the north he suddenly saw something familiar. Far across an undulating slough was an island, in the middle of which rose an ancient, giant spruce that had been topped by lightning early in its growth. Since then two new trunks had grown up out of the central stump, like horns from the head of a bull. They were almost perfectly matched... and unmistakable. Adam started with excitement. He remembered that tree! It was where the winter trail turned downstream toward Fort Yukon, only three or four miles away. His grandfather had pointed it out to him when he was much younger.

Just as he recognized this landmark, Dr. Jackson walked up behind him. "Adam," he asked, "where's my shovel? We can lend a hand. They're trying once more to dig the boat free."

For a second, Adam's heart lurched, then he grinned as he stuffed his hand in his pocket and pulled out a five and two ones. Handing the five-dollar bill to Dr. Jackson he said, "In all the confusion,

I forgot. I got your money back."

"You what?"

"I got your money back for the shovel. You remember. It was your $5 I used to buy it. Well, in Dawson City I sold it, and here's your money."

"But that was *my* shovel," said Dr. Jackson. His voice was quiet, but he was frowning under his derby hat. "You didn't ask me if you could sell it. Do you remember me making a point that the shovel now belonged to me? I told you that you could use it if you asked, but it was mine. You remember?"

"Yes," admitted Adam. He felt terrible. He'd never thought of it like that. He was only trying to make things right by getting Jackson's money back for him. Now the doctor was making it sound like he stole something again.

The doctor put his hand on Adam's arm. "I can see that you didn't intend any wrong. But let me ask you something. I notice you had some more money. Where'd you get that?"

"This?" Adam held up the other two crumpled bills and ventured a grin. "This is my profit. The guy should have paid me more because he was selling shovels for $15, but this is all I could get."

"I see," said Dr. Jackson, frowning again and stroking his pointed beard. "Let me get this straight. You took *my* shovel without asking and sold it for more than I paid for it, and therefore you're thinking the profit belongs to you. Is that it?"

"Well," Adam paused. The whole thing looked different when Dr. Jackson said it that way. "I guess if

82

the shovel belonged to you, then the profits should, too." He handed over the other two dollars.

"Thanks for the offer," said Jackson, making no move to take the money, "but I'm more concerned that you develop a clear respect of other people and what belongs to them. I know you were trying to make things right, but something has clouded your thinking. Do you have any idea what that might be?"

Adam shook his head. This was an uncomfortable conversation. Each time he thought it was over, it took a new turn.

"Let me take a guess," said Dr. Jackson. "Back in St. Michael, I think you caught a little of this gold fever and had ideas of making it big. That's what caused you to lose your way in buying that shovel in the first place. We had that all straightened out, then you had a relapse up there in Dawson. You saw there was another way to make money by being a wheeler-dealer. Again you used something that belonged to someone else for yourself. Does that about account for what happened?"

Adam nodded his head miserably. He could see that what he'd done wasn't right, and it was a relief to have it out in the open. But there was something that still troubled him. In a way he felt like he had only been trying to do the same kind of thing Dr. Jackson was always doing—putting together deals, taking advantage of opportunities. What was the difference?

That evening three canoes of Indians approached the stranded riverboat. They had a few stiff furs with them that they wanted to trade, but they were not interested in blankets or knives or pots. Instead, in urgent sign language they made it clear that they wanted food. The pilot gave them a little and sent them on their way, though he wasn't much interested in their ragged furs.

After that, days of hard work passed as the crew and various volunteers worked on freeing the grounded steamboat, but without success. They even tried to hook a line around a tree on an island back upstream about eighty yards, but when they started pulling on the winch, it just pulled the tree out of the sandy island soil, and it floated down the river.

Finally they decided that without the help of another steamboat to help pull them free or a heavy rain to raise the water, the steamer was stuck fast. They had to go for help. The pilot and a couple deckhands rowed the steamer's little rowboat across from island to island until they were sure they were on the bank of the main channel. There they put up a large blanket between two trees with the word HELP painted on it and an arrow pointing toward the grounded steamboat.

Food was running low on the riverboat, and several passengers complained to the pilot for having traded some of their supplies to the Indians. One afternoon the men tried shooting at the ducks and geese that occasionally flew by. Only four were downed, and they succeeded in retrieving two with the rowboat. By evening any wildlife in the area seemed to have fled.

"No use sitting around here waiting," said the pilot the next morning. "We need more wood for the boiler. When help does come, we've got to be able to do all we can under our own steam." With the rowboat, he dropped teams off at the surrounding islands to cut wood from the snags that were caught on the banks. And that's when the accident happened. The rowboat was overloaded with firewood when it hit a snag hidden under the water in the fast current. The little boat capsized, and the two men who were rowing it saved themselves only by grabbing a couple logs of firewood. The rowboat, however, drifted downstream too fast for anyone to swim after it.

The accident brought many of the passengers to the verge of panic. Now even the rowboat was gone! How were they going to get more food?

That evening more canoes of Indians arrived, again wanting food. The pilot would not let them on board. "No. No food," he said, shaking his head and waving them away.

But the Indians wouldn't take no for an answer. They tossed their bundles of furs up on the deck and began offering other personal items—moccasins, a pipe, a bow and some arrows—to the individual passengers who were leaning over the rail watching the Indians in their canoes.

Suddenly one of the Indians pointed at Adam. "I know you," he said in the Tananan dialect. "You are

Gnob. I knew your grandfather. What are you doing with all these white people?"

"I went to school," Adam said proudly, "far beyond the Nutzotin Mountains, in the land of the Tlingits."

"Then give us food," the man said. "Your own village will be hungry this winter. All the white men have driven off the caribou and the salmon."

"No. We can't. We don't have enough ourselves," explained Adam in his native language. "We have been stranded for days—since the new moon—and our food is nearly gone."

"You are a traitor," the man said with an ugly sneer.

Soon the Indians and the people on board the steamboat were shouting at one another, often not understanding what the other said because of the language barrier. But when the pilot went in and came out with a gun, the Indians grabbed their furs off the edge of the deck and paddled away.

"You are a traitor, Gnob!" yelled the Tananan Indian in his native tongue. "Your grandfather would be ashamed of you."

His grandfather. Surely his grandfather wouldn't be ashamed of him. He'd be proud that his grandson was on the road to becoming a successful man... wouldn't he?

As Adam thought about the old man who had

taught him how to find his way through the vast wilderness, he suddenly remembered the lightning-topped spruce he had seen. "We're not that far above Fort Yukon," Adam said to those left standing on the deck as the Indians paddled away in their canoes. "We could send someone for help."

"We could if we still had our rowboat," said the riverboat pilot. "It would be a job to row that tub back upstream, but by now it would be worth the try... if we had it."

"But the fort isn't upstream," said Adam, glancing at Dr. Jackson to see if he was being too brash contradicting the pilot. But Dr. Jackson didn't scowl, so he went on. "The fort's downstream."

"I doubt it, lad," said the riverboat pilot, still staring after the Indian canoes, which were almost out of sight. "I'm afraid we slipped past the fort in the fog the other night."

"But, sir," Adam said. He glanced again at Dr. Jackson. "I beg your pardon, but my people used to travel through here every winter on our way to Fort Yukon. I recognize that old lightning-struck spruce over there on that island. Our winter trail ran right past it. I'm sure the fort is downstream. Maybe we could build a raft and float down to it."

"I wish that were so," the pilot said tolerantly, "but if wishes were money, we'd all be rich, wouldn't we." He laughed at his little joke. "No. I'm afraid we're below Fort Yukon; we went past it the other night. Anyone going downstream on a raft would have to travel all the way to Beaver before they could find help, and in this maze of islands, that would be suicide. I couldn't allow it."

"But, sir! I recognize that old snag. I know we're above Fort—"

"Son," interrupted the pilot, turning to look at him with an irritated expression, "there are thousands of lightning-topped trees in this country. Things look different in the winter. That tree's not something I'm willing to pin anyone's life on."

That night Adam couldn't sleep. The Indian in the canoe had said his grandfather would be ashamed of him. Now the pilot wouldn't believe him. He had to prove them both wrong. He was certain that Fort Yukon was only a short distance downstream, not upstream. If no one else would go, he would go for help by himself.

Adam got up just before dawn, hours before the other stranded boat people would rise, especially since they had nothing to do but wait. He took a hunting knife and a length of rope and lowered himself over the bow of the paddle-wheeler. Once he had waded to the first island downstream, he gathered as many of the discarded barrels as he could in the tarpaulin and dragged them around to the other side of the island. He didn't want the pilot trying to stop him.

He found two stout poles about twice as long as he was tall, and after smoothing them off with the

88

knife, he laid them parallel on the beach with one barrel at each end holding them apart. These he lashed together as well as he could with rope. Then he wrapped the whole frame with the canvas and tied it tightly. When he tested sitting on the canvas between the poles, it was as though he were riding on a hospital stretcher. But he knew that a small whiskey barrel at each end would not keep him stable in the water, so he tied on four more barrels—two on each side like outriggers.

When he tested sitting on the contraption in the river, he found that his seat sank down into the water, but otherwise it made a very suitable cross between a raft and a kayak. Now all he needed was a paddle. It didn't take long for him to carve a crude one from a driftwood board he found on the island.

All day Adam paddled between the islands, drifting downriver, but he saw nothing. Hour after hour he drove on. His hands were bleeding where blisters had formed, then popped, and finally tore off. Could he have been wrong after all? He was sure he had recognized that tree! But after sitting in icy water all day long, he was so cold that he began shivering uncontrollably. And now the sun was setting, taking with it the summer warmth it provided, and he was being devoured by mosquitoes.

Adam's confidence flagged and he began to feel fear. No one knew where he was. He could die out here and—

Just then the little raft floated around the end of an island, and Adam saw welcome lights flickering on the banks just ahead: Fort Yukon.

As he paddled with the last of his strength over to the town's landing, he called out for help. Luckily willing hands grabbed him and lifted him out of the makeshift raft, because his legs were so numb from the cold that he couldn't walk.

"There she is!" Adam yelled.

Another steamboat on its way downriver, hearing about the stranded *Portus B. Ware* after stopping at Fort Yukon for fuel, agreed to go back upstream looking for it. Adam went along to help guide its pilot. The rescue boat steamed in and out between the many islands, until finally Adam saw the familiar boat listing slightly on its side.

Nineteen days after the *Portus B. Ware* went aground, everyone on board was rescued and again on their way downriver in the rescue boat.

Dr. Jackson embraced Adam with a long hug. Adam could tell that the man's voice quavered with emotion when he whispered in his ear, "I thought you had fallen into the river and drowned, son. I was beside myself. And now to discover that you managed our rescue! Thank God."

Chapter 8

Glory Days

EXCEPT FOR THE CROWDING on the new boat, the remainder of the trip down the Yukon River was uneventful. At St. Michaels on the coast, Dr. Jackson and Adam said good-bye to Mr. Kjellmann, who headed north by boat to the Teller Reindeer Station.

Then they waited for a steamer to take them south to the States. The first one available was the cutter *Corwin*, bound for San Francisco. Adam was disappointed not to see Captain Healy again, but they heard that the *Bear* was far to the north trying to catch some seal poachers.

Two weeks later in San Francisco, Adam's dreams began to come to life. His eyes glowed as he took in the tall buildings, extravagant homes, trolley cars crawling up and down the hills, ships in the harbor, and trains connecting to every part of the country.

Here was the hustle and bustle of American business and social life. To be part of this was what Adam had gone to school for. To make his place in *this* world was his dream.

He also enjoyed the attention that came with Dr. Jackson's reputation as an expert on Alaska. San Francisco reporters wanted Dr. Jackson's view of the gold rush. Did he think there was more gold to be found? Was he intending to stake a claim himself? When would he return to Alaska? Even Adam got interviewed.

But it didn't stop there. When they got off the train a few days later in Denver, Colorado, where Dr. Jackson had to check in with the *Rocky Mountain Presbyterian*, a missionary newsletter for which he wrote, they were immediately approached by two newspaper reporters.

"Dr. Jackson, I'm Frederick Bonfils, and this is Harry Tammen. We're the owners of the Denver Post, and—"

"Ah, yes," said Jackson. "I heard you fellows bought the old *Evening Post* a couple years back. Pleasure to meet you." He reached out his small hand and shook each of theirs in a businesslike manner.

"We were wondering," said Tammen, "if we might take you... and your friend here," he said with a smile that clicked on and then off for Adam. "We'd like to take you to dinner. Would you have time?"

"Be glad to."

"How 'bout the Brown Palace Hotel, then?" grinned Bonfils.

The nine-story hotel, located where Seventeenth Street joined Broadway at a sharp angle, was a magnificent triangular-shaped building. Inside, the atrium rose to a ceiling nine levels above with the guest rooms all around the edge and balconies for each floor. Like the inside of a huge cave glittering with dozens of electric light bulbs, the atrium echoed with the soft voices of guests. Beautiful violin music played in one corner by a tall black man accompanied on the piano by a shorter man with freckles and a very red beard.

Adam had never imagined such grandeur.

For dinner, Adam had the Caesar salad, sliced beef tenderloin with small red potatoes, and a dessert of marinated fruit and berries with grated chocolate on top.

But as soon as the food was delivered, the newspaper men got to their purpose. "Dr. Jackson," said Bonfils, "it's our intention to have the best newspaper in this part of the country. We want to be first with any important story. And that's why we didn't just send one of our cub reporters to talk to you."

Dr. Jackson nodded and wiped the corner of his mouth with his large white linen napkin.

"What we want to know is," put in Tammen, "did you see any evidence of starvation when you were in Alaska this last time?"

"Starvation? No," frowned Jackson as he peered from one to the other through his steel-rimed spectacles. "Well, that is, we did get stranded on a sandbar on our way down the Yukon and ran a little short on food, but other than that, I didn't miss a meal."

"But how about Dawson City? Was food in short supply there?"

"Hmm. Might have been a little tight. The prices certainly were outrageous compared to the States. But what else can be expected when thousands of people rush ill-prepared into the wilderness?"

"Have you heard any reports of a government rescue operation for the miners?"

"The miners? Now, just a minute," said Jackson. "What are you talking about?"

"We're talking about the potential for starvation among the miners—the good citizens of the United States up there in the wilderness," said Tammen.

"You see," said Bonfils in a hushed voice as he leaned forward, "we've received confidential reports that there might not be enough food to see the miners through the winter. So we were wondering if you could comment on that."

"Humph. Don't see how I could comment, since I don't know anything about it," said Jackson.

"Let me put it another way," said Tammen. "From your knowledge of Alaska and what it's like to live through such a long, harsh winter, is there a possibility that the miners could run short?"

"Of course there's a possibility when it comes to

miners," chuckled Jackson. "Anything's possible with those fools. They don't think past tomorrow."

"Then will you be recommending a rescue expedition when you get to Washington, D.C.?" asked Tammen.

Jackson, apparently not wanting to appear ignorant on a subject about which he should have been knowledgeable, said, "If there's a need, certainly. After all, it's my job to look out for Alaska!"

The next day as they hurried to catch their train, Adam tugged on Dr. Jackson's sleeve and pointed to the headline on a newspaper hocked by a small boy on the train platform. It said, "Yukon Miners May Face Starvation!"

"Oh no," groaned Dr. Jackson. "How did they come up with that from what I said?"

At each train stop, Jackson snatched up the daily paper, trying to keep up with the story. By the time the train arrived in Winona Lake, Indiana, all the major newspapers of the country were declaring starvation in the gold fields. Jackson's own words had been exaggerated, but newspapers all across the country were reporting on letters written to families and politicians from miners themselves saying they, too, feared serious shortages.

The Winona Lake paper reported that the secretary of war had sent Captain P. H. Ray of the 8th Infantry to investigate. The reports he sent back confirmed that things didn't look good for the miners, but he also wrote that bands of Indians were already starving. In fact, a few women and children had died on the trail as the tribes tried to reach settlements. One cause of their plight was that the caribou migration had bypassed the Indians' normal hunting grounds—probably because of the large number of miners in the area, Ray said—and the Indians had also suffered a bad salmon run that year.

"This wouldn't be much of a problem," the newspapers reported Ray as saying, "if it weren't for this gold rush. Without the miners in the area, the Indians could simply buy supplies from the trading posts and settlements, but gold-crazed miners will pay any price for supplies. So the supplies that might have helped the Indians have been sold to the miners. It could be a very bad winter, especially with eight to ten thousand eager miners still on their way into the Klondike by way of Skagway and the Chilkoot Pass."

"Hmm. Looks like there may be more trouble than I figured," said Jackson, more to himself than to Adam, after reading the newspaper account. He pushed his spectacles back on his nose. "But I've got an idea. Should have brought William Kjellmann with us, but how could I have known?"

He turned to Adam. "You wait right here," he said, indicating a bench in front of the train station. "I've got to go back in there and send a telegram to William. It'll take a couple weeks to reach him, but I'm going to need his help."

Sheldon Jackson had stopped in Winona Lake, Indiana, to attend the 109th General Assembly of the Presbyterian Church. Again, Adam drank in the sight in amazement. Two thousand representatives had gathered for the convention. When they all got together for their large meetings, the singing literally shook the huge tabernacle building.

The first item of business was to elect a new moderator for the General Assembly and for the whole Presbyterian Church for the following year. To Adam's surprise, Sheldon Jackson was nominated along with Dr. Henry Minton of San Francisco. Then speeches were given supporting each of the candidates. A man named Dr. Spining spoke in favor of Sheldon Jackson, saying, "No man has done more to win this land for Christ than Sheldon Jackson—little Sheldon Jackson. Yes, he may be small of stature, but he is great in spirit."

In another speech, Dr. McMillan, the President of Richmond College in Ohio, said, "I believe Dr. Jackson to be the greatest missionary since Paul. Indeed, he has traveled over six hundred thousand miles in service to God, his church, and his country."

Adam straightened his shoulders proudly. He wasn't surprised when the ballets were counted that Dr. Jackson had won by a large majority. But he was startled when during his acceptance speech, Jackson called Adam up onto the stage before the two thousand representatives.

To keep his knees from shaking when he walked up on the stage, Adam focused on the small stool that

Dr. Jackson was standing on so he wouldn't appear so short. The second thing he noticed was that his mentor's voice sounded louder than he had ever thought possible from such a small man.

"Ladies and gentlemen," boomed Dr. Jackson, "I'd like you to meet a young man who is the product of your care and sacrificial giving. He is the direct fruit of our educational efforts in Alaska. This past summer, he graduated from our Sitka Industrial and Training School, not only as the number one student in his class but as the most outstanding student in all of Alaska. In so doing, he won a prize I had offered to travel with me to the States. I am proud to present... Adam Christian."

The applause was like the roar of the ice pack breaking up in the spring on the Yukon River. Adam felt a rush of excitement mingled with embarrassment creep all the way to his shoes.

"Go ahead, Adam," urged Jackson in a softer voice. "Say something."

By now Adam was standing to the side of the pulpit. "Good evening," he managed to say.

"Louder," said Jackson. "There are a lot of people out there."

"Good evening." Adam felt like he was yelling. "I wanted to come to America because... well, to become like Dr. Jackson, so I studied very hard." He looked around at the field of faces, important people waiting for him to say something important. "I am... very glad to be here." He felt a hot wave of embarrassment crawl up his neck and face at his loss for

words. What he had said seemed dumb to him, but he couldn't think of anything else to say.

Nevertheless, the people clapped as he headed to the edge of the stage and down the steps, hoping that he wouldn't stumble on his shaky legs. Back in his seat in the front row, he was unable to concentrate on anything else Dr. Jackson or the other speakers were saying. Adam kept going over and over his comments, thinking of things he could have said that would have sounded more educated, more like the successful person he wanted to be.

But the rest of that evening and during the next day, Dr. Jackson didn't seem disappointed in Adam, and the doctor eagerly introduced him to everyone he met. Slowly Adam became more comfortable with shaking hands and saying, "How do you do. I'm very glad to meet you." That seemed to be all he was expected to say.

After two days at the General Assembly, they again boarded the train and traveled on to Jackson's home in Washington, D.C., where they arrived on November 1. There was a light snow falling, but his wife and family burst out of the house without their coats to greet him with joy and many hugs.

"Daddy, Daddy," cried the youngest of his three daughters, "are you going to be home now for a long time? We missed you so much. Guess what I made you for Christmas!"

"You've already finished my Christmas present?" Jackson chuckled. "Aren't you the early bird. Oh, my dear girls, it's so good to be home, and yes, I hope to be here for a good long time. But I still have work to do. Tomorrow I've got to report to the secretary of agriculture about the pasturage I found along the Yukon."

"But, Sheldon," Mrs. Jackson said, disappointment creeping into her voice, "must you go in tomorrow? Can't you take at least a few days off?"

"I won't take long," he answered, glancing over the top of his spectacles at his wife. "But I'm working for the president of the United States now—through his secretary of agriculture, of course."

"You used to say you worked for the Lord," Mrs. Jackson said. Adam thought there was a definite frosty edge to her voice. "Who have you decided is greater, Sheldon?"

"Now, now, let's not quarrel, dear," soothed Jackson. He turned to his girls, drew in a deep breath through his nose, and opened his eyes so wide that they almost looked larger than his spectacles. "Guess what, girls! Adam can stay here with you. And the whole family can ask him all about his home in Alaska."

"But, Daddy," said Jackson's oldest daughter, who seemed to be nearly an adult. "We don't care about Alaska. We want you."

Adam saw a disappointed glaze come over Mrs. Jackson's eyes as she turned and went back into the house.

Chapter 9

Journey to the End of the Earth

WITHIN A WEEK, the newspaper headlines were declaring, "Gold Miners Starving Along the Yukon." The editorial columns in the papers demanded that the politicians in Washington do something to rescue them. After all, they were America's fathers, brothers, and sons. They couldn't be left up there in the frozen waste. But no one had any idea how a rescue could be managed. The Yukon River was again frozen solid.

"I'm going to recommend reindeer," said Dr. Jackson one evening around the dinner table. "The Yukon may be frozen, but reindeer could get through. That's why I sent that telegram to William Kjellmann when we stopped in

Indiana—remember, Adam? He'll be in Norway soon, and I told him to buy some of the Lapps' deer. I knew we could use them one way or the other. But now I'm particularly glad I sent him. If I can get Congress to authorize the money to help rescue those miners, we can purchase a whole herd of deer and make a fine showing. What threatens as a tragedy—what with the miners going hungry and all—could be our finest day."

Adam enjoyed staying with the friendly Jackson family. He could tell the girls loved their father and that they envied Adam for the seven long months he'd been spending with the man. They kindly showed him all the sights in D.C. while Dr. Jackson worked hard to get Congress to provide the money to rescue the gold miners. When President McKinley's administration realized the widespread public concern over the "Alaskan crisis," as it had come to be known, Jackson was transferred from answering to the secretary of agriculture to reporting for special duty to General Alger, the secretary of war.

"We've run into a problem," Jackson said one day when he came home. "It seems Hugh Wallace, who is building a railroad to the base of Chilkoot Pass so supplies can be taken over by an aerial tramway, just sent a telegram saying he's quite certain there won't be any starvation in Dawson. If Congress hears that, they may not give us our money."

On December 20, he came home in better spirits. "Congress put up the money, and General Alger has appointed me to carry out this difficult and dangerous mission. I'm to leave at the earliest possible moment."

"Surely not before Christmas?" gasped Mrs. Jackson in despair.

"No, no, of course not." He stopped and counted on his fingers. "This is Monday. Christmas isn't until Saturday, so" —a big grin spread across his small, pointed face— "we'll just have an early Christmas. How about Wednesday, the day before Adam and I leave?" Dr. Jackson turned and slapped Adam on the shoulder. "What do you say, Adam? You up for a trip to Norway?"

"Sheldon, p-l-e-a-s-e," Mrs. Jackson moaned. "How can you do this?"

"My dear, I already told you. It's the miners in Alaska. Congress has authorized $200,000 to purchase and deliver supplies to those miners. Through his secretary of war, President McKinley has asked me to organize the relief expedition. What else can I do?"

"Yes, but why right now? Why you, Sheldon?"

"Because there's no other man with the experience or the vision. And it has to be now because men—even some women and children—may be dying."

The subject was closed.

Early Thursday morning, as Adam and Dr. Jackson were getting ready to leave, Jackson said, "I have to meet with General Alger and do some other business this morning, so there's no real reason for you to come with me now, Adam. I can come back here and pick you up on the way to our train for New York."

Jackson's wife and daughters were standing around in their housecoats and slippers looking forlorn as Sheldon and Adam moved their baggage into the entryway. "On second thought," said Jackson, "you've probably never seen a telephone work, have you, Adam?"

Adam shook his head. He had heard about the "talking wire," but he had never seen one work.

"I have to make a lot of phone calls this morning, so why don't you come along. The horse cab will be here in a few minutes." Then he went from one to the other, kissing and saying good-bye to his wife and daughters. With tears in their eyes, they did not have much to say.

A few hours later, Adam was sitting in Dr. Jackson's office waiting for the little man to come back from his meeting with General Alger when the telephone on Dr. Jackson's desk began ringing. Adam did not know what to do. He had seen Dr. Jackson make several outgoing calls earlier, and it all seemed simple enough. But there had been no incoming calls. Finally Adam picked up the earpiece and listened.

He heard nothing but a hissing and the occasional crackle of static, but he spoke into the speaking instrument as he had seen Dr. Jackson do, "Hello?"

In a thin, tinny voice but with perfectly clear words, he heard a woman say, "I have your New York call for you. Go ahead, please."

Adam was so amazed that he didn't know what to do. Then he heard a man's voice say, "Hello?"

"Hello," said Adam back to him.

"This is the *Lucania* ticket office. What can we do for you?"

"I... I don't know," stammered Adam. "I mean, could you please wait a moment? Dr. Jackson will be here soon."

There. He had done it!

Just then Dr. Jackson came back into the room, peeling off his coat and scarf.

"It's New York," whispered Adam as he pointed to the telephone.

Jackson grabbed the earpiece and sat down at his desk. "Hello. This is Dr. Sheldon Jackson. I'm calling to check on my passage on the steamship *Lucania*. Do you have that confirmed for two passengers?"

He listened and nodded, then said, "Uh-huh... uh-huh.... Yes, we'll be there in plenty of time.... Yes, thank you. Good-bye," while he made notes on a scrap of paper in front of him.

After he hung up, he turned to Adam and said, "It's all set, and you are going to make someone a fine secretary someday. Thank you for taking the call."

Amazing, thought Adam. *I actually spoke to someone in New York, over two hundred miles away, using nothing but a wire to carry my voice.*

At 6:30 on Christmas morning, Dr. Jackson and Adam were settled securely in their cabin aboard the steamship *Lucania* as it backed away from the dock in New York. They were on their way across the Atlantic.

But the night before they sailed, Dr. Jackson had sent a telegram to Mr. Kjellmann in Norway telling him to double his efforts. In part it said,

AUTHORIZE PURCHASE OF 500 REINDEER (STOP) HIRE 50 LAPP HERDERS (STOP) SECURE SLEDS AND ALL EQUIPMENT AND 250 TONS OF MOSS (STOP)

The Luciana arrived in England on the last day of 1897 with Dr. Jackson feeling relieved that his seasickness had not troubled him too much while crossing the Atlantic.

After making further arrangements in London for a steamship to meet them in Norway to pick up the reindeer, Dr. Jackson and Adam continued their journey on January 3 by boat and train through Holland, Denmark, and Norway to the town of Trondhjem, where Jackson purchased 250 tons of reindeer moss for food for the reindeer's return trip.

Then they journeyed by boat to Hammerfest, the northernmost city on the globe—often called the "end of the earth." Again they transferred to a smaller vessel and steamed up the Alten Fjord to the village of Bosekop, where they planned to meet Mr. Kjellmann and pick up the reindeer herd and herders. It was January 13.

This far north, the sun never ventured above the

horizon from November 20 through January 21. When they landed in the gloom of the arctic night, Dr. Jackson said, "Adam, I have to stay here and see that all our luggage gets unloaded from the boat. No one seems to speak English, so I'm not sure they understand my directions. Could you go on up the street and see if you can find a hotel or some place for us to stay?"

In spite of the dark, it was still possible to see... a little. Clouds in the sky and snow-covered earth reflected the wasted remnants of the hidden sun in this blue-black world where only the glow from occasional windows in the small village offered any cheer. In the middle of the day, the light would increase to a dull gray—no more.

Crunching dry snow with every step, Adam made his way up the street trying to see through the frosted panes. Where would he find a hotel in a place like this?

A door slammed, and Adam saw a small figure leave one of the cottages and trudge in his direction. "Excuse me," said Adam when they were within speaking distance. "I'm looking for a hotel... a hotel, a place to sleep. Do you speak English?"

"English a little. Uncle speak English," said the boy who couldn't have been more than a couple years younger than Adam. He beckoned for Adam to follow him back to his house.

It turned out that the house was also the office for the local telegraph operator, and the man spoke fairly good English. As soon as Adam explained his errand, the man said, "Of course. You are the Americans. We are expecting you." He turned to the boy and rattled off some instructions in Norwegian, and the boy went out again.

"My nephew, Mikkel," said the man. "I have sent him for a sleigh to pick up your Dr. Jackson. He and his family will be going with you to America. It is a great opportunity for him to learn English."

Within a few minutes Adam heard bells ringing. "That'll be Mikkel with the sleigh," the man said. "He'll take you to the inn."

Once Dr. Jackson and their luggage had been picked up with Mikkel's reindeer sleigh, the boy drove them to a small two-story hotel. The innkeeper spoke no English, but with Mikkel's broken English, their needs were communicated and they were soon in a cheery room with a good view of the town. The beds were piled high with thick comforters, and they had their best night's sleep since leaving Washington, D.C.

Two days passed, however, and a snowstorm hit, but still Mr. Kjellmann had not come in with the reindeer and the other herders. As the blizzard worsened, it became impossible to see more than a few yards even in the middle of the day, and at night it wasn't even safe to go outside the inn.

"Help me hang this blanket over the window," Dr. Jackson said to Adam. "That howling wind is coming straight in." But they had no sooner secured the top of the blanket when the bottom billowed out like a loose sail.

As Jackson stepped down off the chair on which he had been standing, he suddenly crumpled to the floor with a gasp.

"Dr. Jackson! What's the matter?" cried Adam, rushing to his side.

"Oh, my rheumatism's acting up, and my knee won't hold me," he groaned. "Just help me get to that chair. Being out in the cold so long is what's done it. I should have known better. Could you go downstairs and get the innkeeper to fix me a hot water bottle? If they don't have one, heat some stones on their stove and put them in a blanket. I'll wrap that around my knee. That should help some."

Downstairs, Adam was unable to communicate with the innkeeper. After trying for several minutes, he decided to go get the help of the telegraph operator. Growing up in Alaska, Adam had seen some pretty treacherous weather, but nothing had been worse than this blizzard. He staggered from house to house in the driving wind, almost losing his way several times before he arrived at the telegrapher's cottage.

The man said he couldn't leave at that time because he was expecting some messages from Hammerfest. "Tell you what I'll do," he said in his thick Norwegian accent. "You tell me what your doctor wants, and I'll write it down in Norwegian for the innkeeper to read."

Two hours had passed before Adam brought the heated stones to the lame Sheldon Jackson. "I'd begun to think you were lost in that storm," Jackson said as he carefully wrapped the warmers around his knee.

"If it wasn't for Mikkel, who walked me back here to the inn, I might have gotten lost," Adam said, rubbing his cold ears. "It's terrible out there. I don't know how Mr. Kjellmann can possibly make it. It's gotta be worse up in the mountains."

"I've been worrying about that, too," Dr. Jackson admitted. "And how can any ship possibly navigate that narrow fjord in the dark in weather like this? If the storm doesn't let up soon..." For a moment the man seemed lost in thought. Then he said, "Adam, you and I need to do some serious praying, or this whole project may be lost before it's even started."

Chapter 10

The World Watches

THOUGH DR. JACKSON'S KNEE remained too painful to go outside the hotel on the icy, uneven streets of Bosekop, he insisted on going downstairs for breakfast the next morning. "I have too much to do to let this get me down," he said.

"But there's nothing we can do until the reindeer get here," said Adam.

"Nevertheless, I won't be cooped up in this room. Give me a hand, would you, Adam?"

Together they hobbled down the stairs and sat at a table before the fire as the innkeeper brought them a breakfast of toast, cheese, jam, and strong coffee. "At least they don't serve that stinky fish for breakfast," whispered Dr. Jackson. The innkeeper, not understanding English, nodded and smiled broadly as he served their coffee.

They heard someone stomping his feet on the front stoop, then the door swung open with a blast of wind, and an ice monster—or so it seemed—stood framed against the blue-black storm outside.

"William!" shouted Jackson as he struggled to stand on his one good leg. "Is that you? Are you all right?"

"Yah. It's me... I t'ink," Kjellmann mumbled. He slammed the door and began raking icicles out of his huge black beard. He was covered with snow that soon began melting in the warm room. "You got any coffee, nice and hot? I been on da trail for two days and two nights wit'out no break."

"Sit down. Sit down," Jackson urged. "Adam, get him a chair."

Once Kjellmann began to thaw out with a cup of coffee in his gnarled hands and puddles of melting snow and ice began accumulating on the floor beneath him, he told his story. Over five hundred reindeer were gathered in various herds waiting for the weather to break so they could be brought over the mountains. "The herders are all lined up, too," he said. "We got ten Finns, fifteen Norwegians, and forty-three Lapps signed up, plus all their women and chil'ren."

"What?" said Jackson in shock. "Did you say women and children?"

"Oh yah. Sixteen of dos boys, dey are married

now, and all together—I t'ink I counted—dey got dem nineteen chil'ren. Plus we got plenty sleds and harnesses."

Jackson frowned. "How many?"

Kjellmann pulled a wad of folded papers out of his pocket and a stubby pencil. He carefully unfolded the papers and began counting. "We got us 539 deer, 418 sleds, and 511 sets of harnesses. You t'ink dat's enough?"

"Of course. You did great." Jackson stroked his pointed beard and frowned. "But are you sure they all understand the terms of their contract?" he asked.

"Just like you say," nodded Kjellmann. "Dey signed up for at least two years. Dey get free transportation, light, heat, food, and clothing, and $22.33 a month . . . dat American money. If any choose to stay in Alaska, I tell dem dey will be loaned a herd for t'ree to five years and can keep all da fawns born during dat time."

"And they all agreed?"

"Yah. Dey signed dis paper." He held up the sheet.

"Well, it looks like all we need to do is keep praying that the weather breaks," said Jackson.

"And that the steamship arrives," put in Adam.

"Vhat ship you get?" asked Kjellmann.

"The *Manitoban*. She's an eighteen-hundred-ton iron steamship, with a captain who has sailed the Atlantic for over forty years. We should be in good shape once we get loaded and underway."

Three days later, on February 1, the storm had blown itself out, and several of the herds had made it to town. Once the blue-black of the night gave way to the gray day, Adam went out to see if any more herds had come into town during the night. But before he headed out to the pens, he looked toward the fjord, and there at the end of the street, floating in the black water, loomed the huge hulk of the steamship.

"Dr. Jackson! Dr. Jackson!" yelled Adam as he dashed back into the inn and clambered up the steps three at a time to their bedroom. "The *Manitoban* has arrived—the ship's here!"

That day, with the aid of Adam on one side and a makeshift crutch on the other, Sheldon Jackson made it out of the hotel for the first time in several days and went down to the dock to oversee the construction of the pens that would hold the reindeer on the ship's deck. Meanwhile, William Kjellmann went out to bring in the last of the reindeer and the herders and their families.

Mikkel's parents and little sister were nearly the last to arrive. "I guess you're glad to see them," Adam said to the ruddy-faced boy as they stood on the dock.

Mikkel understood well enough to nod enthusiastically. Then he pointed and said, "Father, mother, sister," designating each of his family members. Like the other Lapp herders, Mikkel's father wore a strange hat that looked like a pillow perched on top of his head with four sharp corners poking out in different directions.

Finally, on February 4, the ship—filled with reindeer, their herders, sleds, and bales of moss—pulled away from the dock and made its way out into the dark sea.

Dr. Jackson, Mr. Kjellmann, and Adam stood at the ship's rail until they could no longer tell the difference between the last twinkling lights along the coast of Norway and the stars in the recently cleared sky. "Well, I'm ready to get belowdeck and see to our stateroom," said Dr. Jackson.

"Yah," said Mr. Kjellmann, "and I tell you, I'm

ready ta t'aw out in my berth. It's been t'ree weeks since I slept in a really warm bed."

But when they got to their "stateroom," it was no more than a storeroom with three bunks. Moisture from the ship's warm air was condensing on the cold steel walls and ceiling like the outside of an icy glass of lemonade in the middle of summer. It dripped from the ceiling and ran down to create puddles on the floor. The bunks were damp and soggy, and everything smelled of mildew. Mr. Kjellmann got no cozy sleep that night, or the next, or the next.

The second day at sea, the sky clouded over and began to release a soft, wet snow that stuck to the deck above. As it slowly melted on the above-freezing deck, the three travelers discovered that the ceiling of their room also had several leaks. Soon water was sloshing back and forth across their floor with the ship's gentle roll.

The pitch of the sea increased as the storm grew, until Dr. Jackson said, "I'm feeling a little green around the gills. It seems to always happen to me on the open sea. Think I'll go up on deck for a little fresh air. Would you come with me, Adam, in case my knee acts up again?"

But up on deck, they found that many of the Lapps were very seasick, and the faint smell of their vomit pushed Dr. Jackson over the edge, causing him to hurry for the side of the ship, as well.

By the sixth day of the trip, the storm had become so severe that waves began breaking over the deck, threatening to destroy the reindeer pens and wash the animals into the sea. Hail and snow continued as the ship smashed through the high seas. Adam overhead the captain say that in all his years of sailing the North Atlantic, he had never seen such a violent storm.

By this time, the water in the travelers' "stateroom" was ankle-deep and as cold as the North Sea.

For nine days the tempest pounded them, driving the creaking steamer to within one hundred miles of Iceland and dashing it into floating icebergs until the ship's prow was broken, its sides battered, and the lifeboats crushed. All the while, everyone but the most hardy sailors suffered violent seasickness.

Then one afternoon Dr. Jackson met Adam coming up from belowdeck hoping to make it to the ship's rail before his stomach kicked back the little soup he had managed to get down. "You look rather green, my boy," the little man said jovially.

"Yes, sir," Adam mumbled, not understanding the doctor's lighthearted tone. "What's happening?"

"Oh, didn't you know?" he said. "The captain thinks the storm is blowing itself out, and we've lost only one reindeer, and that one died from injuries suffered in a fight—not the storm. Those beasts are amazing, aren't they? They were on that deck through the whole storm. It's a miracle, I tell you."

Adam staggered toward the edge of the ship. It was true. As he clung to the rail, he could see that the waves weren't as high, and some of the clouds seemed to be breaking apart. He looked at the pens of sea-soaked reindeer, looking like miserable, overgrown wet rats. It truly was remarkable that they had survived.

After twenty-three days at sea, the *Manitoban* tied up to a pier at Sandy Hook, the entrance to Lower New York Bay.

As soon as they docked, Adam accompanied Dr. Jackson down the gangplank to make arrangements for unloading the deer. Their feet no sooner hit solid wood than a group of reporters rushed them, calling them "the heroes of the gold fields." Once again, Adam felt the sweet taste of fame and attention flood through his whole body.

"This is Adam Christian," Dr. Jackson said, introducing Adam after he had answered a few of the reporters' questions. "He's one of my boys from my schools in Alaska. He went all the way to Norway with me to get these reindeer." He gestured toward the ship where a large, antlered deer was being lowered to a holding pen on the dock by a sling from a ship's derrick, and started to turn away.

"Dr. Jackson! Dr. Jackson!" the reporters protested. "Could you answer a few more questions for us?"

Jackson held up his hand to stop them, then ushered Adam far enough away so they could talk without being overheard. "Adam," he said nervously, "I've got to get back to Washington right away. An Army officer is scheduled to join Mr. Kjellmann to take these reindeer cross-country. The Lapps, of course, will go along on the train, and between them and William, they know what the deer need. But I was wondering, would you be willing to go with them? There are a lot of things you could help with along the way, and this might be the best way for you to get back to Alaska. I'm not sure when I'll be able to make it, and I don't want you to be stranded here indefinitely."

Adam's mind raced. It was an honor for Dr. Jackson to want his help delivering the deer, but he had hoped to spend more time in the States. On the other hand, staying with the reindeer was a way to stay in the action. Newspaper reporters had greeted them as heroes, saying they were risking their lives to save America's brothers and cousins and uncles and, yes, some women, too, who had gone north to Alaska seeking their fortunes.

He had to decide quickly. Should he go or ask to stay with Dr. Jackson? Finally he said, "All right. I'll go with the reindeer. They may need my help in Alaska, and I know Yukon country better than Mr. Kjellmann or anyone else along."

"That's the spirit," said Dr. Jackson as he walked with Adam back to the reporters.

"Gentlemen," he said in his grand, sweeping way. "You've met my boy, Adam Christian. You can ask him anything about Alaska or the expedition you want, but I'm sorry, I can't take any more time with you. I must be going." And with that, he headed back up the gangplank to collect his belongings from the ship.

The questions from the reporters came at Adam

like a hailstorm. "What was it like growing up in Alaska?" "Is there any gold near your village?" "Do you think many miners have died yet?"

"I don't know how many miners might have died by now," he said, "but we are doing everything we can to save them." Yes, he thought that was a good answer.

A reporter dressed in a white shirt with garters on his sleeve, plaid suspenders, and a plaid slouch hat pushed to the front of the group, his pencil poised above a small tablet. He wore spectacles almost like Dr. Jackson's. "Tell us what Sheldon Jackson, the man, is really like," he said. "All we see are the headlines, but day to day, how does he get so much accomplished?"

Adam thought about the question for a moment and then said, "Well, he never sits around, but on the other hand, I've never seen him hurry. He just keeps at a thing until he accomplishes it."

"He does so much traveling. Does he like to travel?"

In his mind, Adam could see Dr. Jackson retching into a bucket or over the rail. "I don't think so, but I've never heard him complain, and he always has time to help other people."

"What do you mean?" asked another reporter. "Give us an example."

Adam knit his forehead, thinking. "Well, on the crossing in the middle of the storm, Dr. Jackson was as sick as the rest of us, but one night he sat down with some of the Lapp children—their parents were even sicker, so sick they could hardly care for their kids—and he cut out paper dolls with a small pair of folding scissors he carries in his pocket. It helped cheer them up."

When the reporters left, Adam thought about the things he had said about Dr. Jackson. He realized that he had been just like the reporters, paying attention only to the headlines and dramatic things Jackson did. But there was more to the man. Jackson had his problems—pushing all the time to get things done, trying to get publicity for his projects, not spending enough time with his family—but his heart was inclined to help people. *What is really my goal?* wondered Adam. *Do I want to help people, like Dr. Jackson... or do I just want some of that glory for myself?*

For the first time in a long time, Adam thought about his family—his grandfather, mother and father, and little brothers and sisters—and the rest of the people in his village. *I wonder,* he thought uneasily, *if they have enough food?*

Chapter 11

Stuck in Skagway

COUPLED BEHIND THE THREE passenger coaches of the special gold miners' rescue train were fifteen cattle cars carrying reindeer, flatcars stacked with sleds, and finally several boxcars for moss, baggage, and other supplies. The caboose *clickety-clacked* at the end of a very long train. At each stop across the country, townspeople gathered along the tracks to get a glimpse of the famous expedition, and local reporters flashed their cameras and asked the same old questions.

When the train stopped in Chicago, Adam walked along the platform to stretch his legs. Peeking curiously into the boxcars at the end of the

train, he was startled to find two of them empty. "Mr. Kjellmann!" he cried, running back to the passenger cars, "I thought those boxcars at the end of the train had reindeer moss in them—but two are empty. Only one has moss! I don't think we have enough feed to last until we get to Alaska!"

"No, no. You must be mistaken. T'ree of dem back cars have moss," Kjellmann said. "Dat's vhat I asked for, and dat's vhat I got."

"I don't think so," said Adam. "Two are empty, and the third one has already been dug into quite a bit. It won't last."

Kjellmann's bushy black eyebrows knit together to make one dark line. "You sure, boy?" he aksed. Seeing that Adam was very serious, the Norwegian turned and trotted toward the back of the train, with Adam close behind. After yanking open the doors of the boxcars, Kjellmann kept mumbling, "Dat's bad! Very bad! Very bad! How can dis be?"

When they told the army officer in charge of the train, he shrugged. "Can't help you, boys. My job's to get this train to Seattle and see that those blooming deer are put on a ship for Alaska. Feeding 'em's your job."

Kjellmann and Adam hurried into the station. "You got one of dem telephones?" Kjellmann demanded of the stationmaster. In a few minutes he was talking to someone at the dock at Sandy Hook, New York. "You did what wit' da moss?... Okay, okay, but we are in bad trouble now! Very bad trouble!"

He hung up with a shocked look on his face. "Half da moss got soaked wit' sea water, so dey t'rew it away and only sent da good stuff wit' us," he said to Adam, his shoulders sagging dejectedly. "We have to put dos deer on half rations for the rest of the trip."

Adam was worried. What if the reindeer starved to death before he and Mr. Kjellman got them to Alaska? Dr. Jackson wouldn't blame them—he'd understand about the moss—but the reporters and the newspapers might not understand. Overnight, what had been described as a "glorious expedition" might turn sour as the press blamed those involved—him included—for foolishly wasting the public's money.

In Seattle, the problem got worse. The ship that was to take them to Alaska had not yet arrived. "We're nearly out of moss," said Mr. Kjellmann, shaking his head. "We gotta save some of it for da voyage to Alaska."

"What if we let them graze on the grass in the city parks?" asked Adam. He, too, was feeling desperate.

"Ha! How would we ever get permission for dat?"

"I don't know," said Adam. "But I'm sure Dr. Jackson could."

Mr. Kjellmann threw his hands into the air. "Yah! He can do 'bout anyt'ing, I guess. *You* call him on dat talking phone, den. It's him dat got us into dis mess in da first place."

Adam didn't know what to do. Obviously Mr. Kjellmann was very upset. But should he call? How would he pay for the call? Finally he told the man at the train station that Dr. Sheldon Jackson in Washington, D.C., would pay for the call.

Surprisingly, it worked. In a half hour he was telling Dr. Jackson the whole story.

"The park grass sounds like the only thing to try," said Dr. Jackson. "I'll make a few calls to see if I can get the parks opened up for you."

No one liked the idea of feeding the reindeer on fresh green park grass, especially not the Lapp herders. They had seldom seen reindeer eating straight grass. But there was no other option. They had to try something.

But after four days on park grass, they realized it was a mistake. The deer became sick and two died. Again, Adam used the telephone at the Seattle station to contact Dr. Jackson. "What should we do?" he asked. "They're saying it will be four more days before the ship gets here, then it'll take a day to get the deer loaded. I don't think they can last that long."

"Ask Mr. Kjellmann about alfalfa," asked Dr. Jackson. "Maybe they could tolerate dry hay better than the fresh grass. You know, too much green grass can make horses and cows sick if they aren't used to it."

"I'll ask him," said Adam, "but... I sure wish you were here."

"I've already rearranged my responsibilities," said Dr. Jackson, "I'll be on this afternoon's train. Hopefully I'll catch you before you sail for Alaska."

To Adam's relief, Dr. Jackson arrived in Seattle on March 16, just as the sick deer were being loaded onto a steamer. The voyage took eleven days traveling up the coast of Canada, weaving through the maze of islands and channels before they arrived at Haines, Alaska, some 150 miles north of Sitka, where Adam had gone to school. Haines was the only southeastern port in Alaska with trails into the interior. Most of the gold miners used the nearby town of Skagway as their launching point over the Chilkoot Pass into Canada and on to the gold fields.

As soon as they arrived and had driven the ailing deer to Skagway, Mr. Kjellmann departed to take up his previous responsibilities that he had so long neglected at Teller Station. Dr. Jackson, Adam, and the Lapp herders—none of whom could speak much English—were left at Skagway to care for 526 weak and starving reindeer.

Life in Skagway was just as Adam had heard, only worse. There was plenty of work if one wanted it. Hundreds of Tlingit Indians—men, women, and even children—worked as packers carrying a ton of supplies per miner up over the 3,739-foot summit. This amount of supplies was now required by the Canadian Mounties before allowing any miner to enter Canada in an attempt to stave off the threatened starvation everyone had been talking about. At certain places the trail was so steep that a man crawling up it on his hands and knees was practically in a vertical position. Steps had been chopped into the ice to keep from slipping back down.

Adam was glad he had not gone to work for the miners, no matter how much it might have paid.

The town of Skagway also boasted eighty-some saloons, though it offered very little sleeping space. The "hotel" Adam and Dr. Jackson finally found was a leaky tent, and their "room" was an old army blanket hung between their bunk bed and the next one. The muddy streets were even worse than those in Dawson. No wonder some said it was little better than hell on earth.

But the worst problems were the would-be miners themselves. They were men with a fire in their belly to get to the gold that hadn't yet been dampened by the reality of wilderness hardships. They thought they could do anything; they would do anything to get their stake, and took out anyone who got in their way. Mix in the con-artists, thieves, and gamblers intent on taking their money before they got to the Klondike, and it was a recipe for trouble.

Every evening there was angry shouting, fights, even gunshots. The poor Lapps, who had set up their tents near the edge of town where the reindeer were penned in a burlap corral, were horrified by these rough, uncouth Americans.

Fortunately for them, nursing the sick reindeer gave them very little time to explore Skagway and its crowded, dangerous streets. The moss for the deer had run out, and the animals were sickening and dying on their diet of dry alfalfa. New pasture had to be found immediately.

"I don't want to attempt moving the deer over the Chilkoot Pass," said Dr. Jackson. "Half of them can't even stand up. They would clog the trail for days. With all those gold miners still climbing the trail, we'd start a riot if we hindered them from getting to their precious gold fields."

In their small bunk space, he looked at Adam who was sitting on the edge of the lower bunk, elbows on knees, chin in hands, staring at the dirt floor. "Adam, is there any other way to get over the mountains than Chilkoot Pass or White Pass?" Chilkoot Pass and White Pass were essentially two branches of the same trail, only a couple miles apart.

Adam nodded. "You can go the western route up the Chilkat River. I used to come that way every year from Tanana. But that's all by foot." He knew the miners elected the route over Chilkoot Pass because on the other side they could build boats to launch in the series of narrow lakes—once the ice had thawed—which took them to the headwaters of the Yukon River. From there, it was nothing but a wild ride all the way to Dawson.

"But can we drive the reindeer up the Chilkat River?" Jackson pressed.

"As long as the ice holds, it's fairly easy going. But once it breaks up..." Adam shrugged. "It's been pretty warm lately."

"Would you check it out?" asked Dr. Jackson. "If we don't get these reindeer to some higher ground where they can find moss, they're all going to die."

It was true. Dozens of deer were dying daily by this time, and the whole project was in danger of failing.

First thing the next morning, Adam caught a boat back down to Haines, crossed the little peninsula of land in the bay, and caught another boat up to

Klukwan, where the open water of the bay ended. Above Klukwan, the Chilkat, Kelhini, Little Salmon, and Tsirku Rivers were still frozen over, though the ice looked brownish gray with the first signs of rot. A thaw was coming soon, and when it did, travel would be nearly impossible.

By foot Adam headed up the Chilkat River Valley. All afternoon he trudged through old, crusted snow. Sometimes its surface was solid enough to support him wearing only his boots, and other times he sank above his knees and had to put on snowshoes to make any headway.

It was dark when he finally arrived at the head of the valley, and he set up a small camp on the shore of the frozen river. The sky was cloudy, and a warm wind blew up the valley, bringing with it the scent of salt water and the sea some twelve miles behind him.

Adam sat with his back to a tree with a small fire at this feet. Over it bubbled a pot of beans. It had been a long time since he had been alone in the wilderness. What was today? April 3, 1898... Palm Sunday. A lot had happened since his graduation from the Sitka school. He had traveled to the other side of the world, seen sights none of his tribespeople had ever dreamed of, and been interviewed as though he were an important person.

If we can get these deer to those miners at Dawson, that would be a real accomplishment, thought Adam, *and I've been part of it the whole way. Maybe I've already traveled the first mile down the road to becom-*

ing an important person like Dr. Jackson. "Success" seemed just around the next bend.

Suddenly Captain Healy's words seemed to pop in his ears along with the crackling fire. *What was it he had said about success?* Adam thought. *Something about not forgetting my own people.* And then he remembered. Captain Healy had said, *"They need everything you have learned in school, or ever will learn. That's real success!"*

But what did that have to do with traveling around the world and being interviewed by newspaper reporters or given important responsibilities like checking out this route for Dr. Jackson? When this expedition was finished, the whole world would know who Adam Christian was. Every door would be open.

Suddenly the crackling of the fire was drowned out by a loud popping sound, a creaking and grating, and more popping. Adam knew what it was.

The ice was breaking up.

There would be no easy trip up the river on top of smooth ice with a herd of reindeer. In fact, it might be days before they could travel this way!

Chapter 12

"Maybe for This You Were Born"

MORE THAN THE ICE on the Chilkat River had broken up with the warm breezes of Palm Sunday. When Adam got back to Skagway, he learned that a snow pack had broken loose from the mountain above Sheep Camp on the Chilkoot Trail, and an avalanche had roared down the mountain, burying seventy men. So far, no one had been dug out alive.

"It could have been us up there with our reindeer," said Dr. Jackson. "We wouldn't have had a chance."

They were both looking out of their third-floor window in the Golden North Hotel with its red, onion-shaped Russian-styled roof on its corner tower. Dr. Jackson had finally managed to get them a *real* room in this newly built hotel. Lined up on muddy Broadway Street below were the bodies of men who had been recovered from the avalanche, each covered with a blanket.

It was a bone-chilling sight.

"There's something else I have to tell you," said Dr. Jackson. "I received a telegram this morning calling me back to Washington."

Adam looked at him in dismay. "But... but why? We're so close to getting the reindeer to the miners. Why quit now?"

"That's just the point. Apparently Captain Ray, that army officer who was up the Yukon investigating the situation, has returned to Washington saying that supplies have gotten through, and no miners are starving. It seems the crisis has passed."

"W-what? But... but what about the reindeer?"

"I'm going to turn the project over to a government man I met here in Skagway, name of Hedley Redmyer. He speaks a little Norwegian, so that will help in communicating with the Lapps. But there's something I'd still like you to do, Adam." Jackson pushed his little derby hat up on his forehead and frowned in his hawklike fashion. "I want you to go along as a guide. It seems no one around here knows the trail up the Chilkat and over the mountains better than you. I want you to take the deer beyond Dawson, all the way to Circle City on the Yukon. If it's true that they're not needed there by the miners, take them down to the mission at Tanana. We'll use them for transportation in the winter."

Adam could hardly believe what he was hearing. "But what about the Lapp herders?" he asked weakly.

"So many reindeer have died we don't need all those herders. I'm planning to send most of them to other reindeer stations. But I'll make sure you have enough to take the deer over the mountains."

Adam felt numb. Dr. Jackson didn't appear that disturbed by the change in events, but to Adam, it seemed that his dreams were slipping from his grasp. The next four days were spent arranging for the transfer of the unneeded Lapp herders. Other herders climbed the surrounding mountains to gather what moss they could find to feed the stranded deer.

On April 8, Dr. Jackson departed Alaska, leaving the transfer of the reindeer in the care of Hedley Redmyer, with Adam to act as guide.

The reindeer were still too weak to travel. With time to kill, Adam climbed up to Sheep Camp on the Chilkoot Trail where the avalanche had occurred. Maybe it was the natural curiosity to see the site of the accident. Maybe he just needed time to think. He didn't really know.

Men were still digging out trapped bodies, but there was no longer any urgency. After six days there wouldn't be any survivors in the snowbank. Work proceeded slowly because of too few volunteers. Most people in Skagway were either on their way to the gold fields or making money off those who were.

As Adam watched, one of the diggers seemed familiar to him. The man's back was to Adam as he shoveled, but the large shoulders, the short black hair streaked with gray, the dark, weathered neck... there was something about the way the man moved, rolling from side to side as he worked as though he were on the deck of a ship.

Then the man slammed his shovel straight down into the snow and turned sideways—

"Captain Healy!" Adam yelled as he leaped over a huge chunk of ice and ran toward him.

The man turned toward Adam, squinting and wiping his huge walrus mustache with the back of his hand. "Adam!" he grinned. The lines in Healy's face were etched deeper, as though he had aged ten years. "I thought you'd be a businessman in Philadelphia by now."

"What are you doing here?" Adam asked, gulping cold air. "Is the *Bear* in port at Haines?"

A pained look crossed Healy's face. "No," he said. "I lost the *Bear*. You were right about the court-martial. They took away my license." He stared far down the mountain toward the sea as though he were looking back in time. "But I stopped drinking," he said with a wry grin, looking again at Adam. "Not a drop in three months."

"That's good," said Adam. "I think you're doing right."

"Yeah, me too." Healy looked around at the work on the avalanche. "Came back up here to Alaska, I guess, 'cause the North feels like home to me, and I thought I'd help out on this disaster work." He shrugged. "How 'bout you? What you doin' these days?"

Shrugging, Adam explained about the gold miners' rescue, and the fact that it no longer seemed needed, but that he was still going to guide the deer to the interior when they got strong enough to travel.

"Hmm. You disappointed?" Captain Healy asked.

"It's like the whole thing never happened!" Adam burst out, for the first time putting his feelings into words. "One day we were the heroes of the world, newspaper reporters taking our pictures and asking us questions. And now... it's all over, and no one seems to care."

Healy gave a short laugh. "That's the way with fame—here today, gone tomorrow. But how 'bout *your* people? How did they survive this past winter? I hear it was a nasty one up there."

Adam remembered the words of his tribesman when the *Portus B. Ware* was grounded on the sandbar. The man had said his people were starving—and that was last summer. "I 'spect they got kind of hungry," he admitted.

"Well," Healy said, "maybe it was for this you were born."

"What do you mean?"

"You're headed up that way with a bunch of reindeer, aren't you?"

"Yes."

"You ever read the story of Esther in the Bible? She became queen of a great empire. She could have looked down her nose on her people, the lowly Jews. But she realized God put her in the palace to save her people in their day of trouble. Said it was for this that she'd been born."

Captain Healy didn't have to spell it out. Adam knew what he was saying. Maybe his going to school, winning the scholarship, traveling with Dr. Jackson, ending up with a reindeer herd in his hands—maybe it all had a different purpose than he'd thought.

The captain laid his hand on Adam's shoulder. "Think about it," he said. "Your people may need you more than you realize."

It took several weeks before the weak reindeer could be led up the Chilkat River Valley, over the mountains, and onto the north slopes where there was an abundance of moss. The herd had suffered a tremendous loss from the 538 that had come across the Atlantic, but Adam, Hedley Redmyer, and the Lapp herders allowed the 144 deer that had survived to graze on the rich moss in an attempt to gain full strength.

Adam had plenty of time to think. Sure, he'd read the story of Queen Esther. He'd read the whole Bible while in school. If he was honest with himself, there were a whole lot of stories in the Bible where the person who tried to be important fell flat on his or her face, while the people who just tried to do what God wanted them to do... well, sometimes they became important people and sometimes they didn't. Like Dr. Jackson. Adam didn't think he set out to become a famous man; it just happened because of all the ways he tried to help the people of Alaska.

Maybe, Adam thought, I ought to talk Redmyer into heading straight for St. James Mission. Forget the miners. Healy's probably right. My people need these reindeer more than those gold-hungry prospectors do.

But then Adam remembered the fiasco with the shovel. He'd gotten himself in a lot of trouble taking things into his own hands. Dr. Jackson had said to take the deer to Circle City, then on to St. James Mission. He'd better do what he'd agreed to do.

Finally the deer seemed to be strong enough to continue the journey, and no more had died. And yet, as they traveled north once more toward the Yukon River, every couple days the count went lower... 142... then 140... 139... 135. But the strange thing was, the deer were just gone. Disappeared.

The Lapp herders thought it was wolves who came in at night and took the weaker animals. But secretly, Adam didn't think so. Certainly, wolves could be heard howling in the woods, and maybe a few kills could be attributed to animals. But when wolves made a kill, there was always plenty of sign, not only of their paw prints but of the bones and scraps of hide they left behind.

But most of the losses on the way to the Yukon were clean—a little blood at most. It was as though a great eagle had come down from the sky and snatched the deer away... or, thought Adam, maybe a human could take a deer at night, drag it away, and come back and brush away the tracks.

He said nothing. The reindeer had been brought to Alaska to help feed hungry people. If the thirty deer they ultimately lost on the drive across Alaska had helped feed his people, so be it. He would finish the task he'd been given, and maybe by the time they got to St. James Mission, there'd be enough reindeer left to start a herd. He'd never thought about being a reindeer herder. But maybe he could develop the herd and help Father Chapman with his little school.

The white mountains of the Yukon River Valley sparkled in the crisp Alaskan spring. *Maybe for this I was born,* he thought, grinning to himself at Captain Healy's words. Funny thing, deep down, he finally felt a strange sense of purpose and peace.

More About Sheldon Jackson

SHELDON JACKSON was another of those missionaries who was at first turned down by his church's foreign mission board, in his case because he was "lacking in physique." That is, they thought he was too small. But he determined to show them. After graduating from Princeton Theological Seminary in 1858 at the age of twenty-four and marrying Mary Voorhees, he threw his heart and soul into "home missions" for the Presbyterian Church, which he extended—in time—to Alaska, an area many considered "foreign" territory.

After ten years working as a teacher in a Choctaw Indian school in Oklahoma and then in Minnesota, he went into general church work in the West, including Colorado, Wyoming, Montana, Utah, and Arizona.

Then in 1877 he visited Alaska and saw the desperate need for education and opportunity for ministry through church-sponsored schools.

However, it soon became apparent that this undertaking would require more money than the Presbyterians or other denominations could provide. In 1884 Jackson lobbied successfully for the "Organic Act," which provided Alaska with a U.S. district court, a marshal, a district attorney, four commissioners, and federal aid for education. Jackson then nominated himself and received appointment from President Grover Cleveland as the general agent for education in Alaska.

Now he had the authority, the money, and the personnel (through church mission organizations) to plant or expand schools throughout Alaska.

Subsequently, several churches adopted Jackson's suggestion to coordinate their efforts in Alaska by not competing for or overlapping territory. The Presbyterians took responsibility for southeastern Alaska and Point Barrow, the Episcopalians—the valley of the Yukon, the Baptists—Kodiak Island and Cook's Inlet, the Methodists—the Aleutian and Shumagin Islands, the Moravians—the interior valleys of Kusko Kwim and Nushkagak, and the Congregationalists—Cape Prince of Wales. This was a remarkable achievement in Christian cooperation in missions.

In addition to his concern for education and missionary cooperation, he also helped set up a postal service for remote areas, campaigned for local government, and encouraged agricultural development. In response to the threat of famine among the Eskimos due to excessive whale and seal harvesting, he introduced reindeer from Siberia and Lapland.

At times the reindeer projects were very controversial. When it looked as if they would be needed to save the Klondike gold miners, many in the States declared him a hero. When they proved unnecessary, he was criticized for foolish extravagance. But the reindeer were successful in that they ultimately thrived in the region and became essential in the economy and diet of many native peoples.

Jackson supervised Alaskan missions for the Presbyterians from 1884 through 1907 and was elected moderator of the whole Presbyterian Church in 1897. He died at home in 1909.